The Alligator's Labyrinth

Julie Buckingham

1

Psychic Red-head, 30 year old Janella Black, bunched her red tapered fingernails together and prayed hard. "Number 15," she squealed in her mind, "make it number 15!"

The ball rolled, the dice spun into orbit around the robotic roulette wheel. Time stopped, as those who played at the Casino table held their breath to see where the dice would eventually slow on this wheel of fortune for the winners and losers of the night. As it spun the roulette ball board flicked numbers on and off, adding to the growing tension of those wondering where it would stop.

For Janella the thrill and uncertainty of waiting for her number to come up made her insides melt. She was a compulsive gambler with the habit strongly ingrained in her psyche. She already owed this club several chits in lost winnings, which is why she and her boyfriend had rowed, and she'd come here again in hot pursuit of her favorite habit, having left her underworld water home for the surface of her planet Deitto.

Closing beautifully mascaraed amber eyes, she looked inward using her medium's sixth sense, searching for the future of the next few moments, to see if she was going to be lucky this time.

She was a Deittonean, born on the surface of this small planet, but because Deitto was heating up, whole homes and cities had been built of glass corridors extending for miles below the sea, the entrance being gained from riding in shunter-taxis throughout many reinforced glass tube-like corridors with their exits marked by shoreline caves all over the planet.

Deittoneans still worked on the surface, but many lived underwater from the heated furnace of the land, which made the sky flush a brilliant crimson at night. Underwater oil reservoirs supplied heating and cooking needs to every household via pipelines entwined inside the glass tunnels with several outlet stations situated at intervals along the way, for the maintenance of the system.

This casino she was in was actually on the surface, and night-time was cooler than the day.

As she closed her eyes the casino's bright lights dimmed behind her eyelids as she willed her number to show up on the board, and the chiming of slot machine games, and ringing and humming of people's talk abated around her as she stood in trance state, inside her own mind-willed darkness, with her fingers now tightly crossed.

Instead of seeing her number win as she had hoped, she saw herself in her trance making a hover-train journey from her flat in Farseisia, under planet Deitto, to the Capital City, which was on the surface, complete with baggage, which suggested to her some future travel of some kind. Her third eye saw herself arriving at a smart mews-type house in the Capital called Jaggard Mews. She could see the name plate clearly etched in electronic black hanging beside the mews door.

Someone jogged her arm. A foreign man's voice said: "Sorry Madam, could you move away? This is my spot; I was here before you, an' I don't like being crowded out! Thank you!"

It was a rich, cultured voice. His dialect suggested he was an Amisanean from the Big Country of Amisana, which lay deep in the ocean across the vast patch of sea from her own birth country of Bretan, which lay in the south east.

She opened her eyes still partly in a trance state, and spied the man who had just spoken to her in vision mode.

He was of medium height, handsome, with wavy 'sunshine' hair and a winsome, flourishing, slightly mysterious smile, deep grooved cheeks and soft green eyes that shone like the ocean sea on a calm day. She was instantly struck by his laid-back attitude and frankly admiring stare, even though his words made her angry.

"You know what? I think you're a rude man! I'm allowed to stand where I want to!"

"I believe I was here first, ma'am!"

"I didn't notice! I was too intent on willing my number to come up!"

"Ah, you're a hooker, right?"

Before she could stop herself her hand drew back and she smartly slapped his face.

"How dare you! I'll have you thrown out of here for using indecent language against me!"

Several people crowding around the casino table moved warily away from them, sensing a row, staring and gesturing.

The man ruefully held a hand to his cheek. "Ouch, lady! What was that for?"

"I'm no hooker, mister!"

"Honey, we've gotten off on the wrong foot! I didn't mean that kinda hooker! I meant you are hooked on this game, is all!"

Seething inwardly and noticing those people around them giving them attentive looks, she brought her temper under control, still thinking him rude, but replied coolly with a fixed smile and a lowered voice, she hissed: "What if I am? I still have the right to be here too!"

He heard the defiance in her voice and matched it with his own. "So3 do I ma'am, but I'm sorry I used the unfortunate word, 'hooker'. It's not one I've used for many years; please accept my mistake an' my churlishness. Can we be friends? I'm willing to bend my rules for a beautiful woman!"

Slightly mollified, Janella said tightly: "Sure, accepted, but I was here first, I believe."

As she spoke she glanced at the roulette wheel. Number nine had showed up on the glow-board that robotic-ally called the numbers. She sighed. She hadn't won.

"Then I couldn't have noticed you, I beg your pardon!"

Janella nodded, she added, conversationally, because he was very rugged and handsome: "Actually, I'm just leaving. I'm waiting for my number to come up! Getting no luck tonight, unfortunately!"

"Don't leave on my account, sweetheart. The evening's young!" He was giving her another appraising glance.

Janella smiled, yet realized she was still in a trance state that took in the gaming room and the stranger beside her.

She found to her shock, she'd fastened on some kind of a man-being, extremely tall and ugly-looking, that quickly moved away from the suited, suave, distinguished man who stood facing her. Also, there was another similar being emerging from under the roulette table who blithely made a sudden exit when it realized she had seen it!

She frowned and gasped out loud. Was she seeing things? It appeared only she could sense these two beings with her second sight!

It had been some kind of alien creature standing behind the man, a tall, irregular-looking thing with an alligator's face that had crinkled menacingly at her. Yet IT had had arms and legs!

And she could have sworn it had red eyes!

She'd never seen it's like before, nor wanted to see it again. It had shaken and frightened her, and she got the distinct impression it had been stalking the man who had just spoken to her.

She blinked and her spooky, creepy feeling of danger vanished.

The man had heard her gasp. As she blinked, clearing her second sight, he asked abruptly with kind concern: "Hey, what's up? You've gone sheet-white! Gee, what a louse I am to speak sharply to you like that! Here, ma'am, d'you wanna sit down?"

"God, I think I've seen some kind of ghost – or ghosts!"

"Yeah? Sorry about my indifference lady – I'll fetch a seat for you!"

Her bare arm was held and he snapped his fingers with a determined flourish as a floating chair came to rest by her side. He helped her into it carefully, seeing how shocked she looked.

"I've ordered you a lug of bourbon!" A fluted, thick tumbler was thrust into her hand. "Drink this, sweetheart. You're as pale as my white crop-top under my expensive suit, which cost me a million in tax money!"

She found her voice. "You look like a millionaire! Thanks. Are you having anything?"

"A lug of bourbon too. Yeah, I kinda like the stuff you drink over here! Cheers ma'am."

They both drank the bourbon quickly as it had been handed to them by an actual waiter and not a robot.

Colour flooded Janella 's face and she regained her suntanned look.

"How d'you feel now ma'am?"

"Better. Thanks for the bourbon, I needed it! I'm Janella Black."

"Hi Janella, I'm Rob McKen."

"Hi."

They shook hands carefully. Her new escort was charming in an Amisanean way, and he was grinning ruefully, as though being cautious about something and being careful not to antagonize her again!

"You say you saw some ghost, or alien being's in here? C'mon, honey, was it real, that's sure sounds unusual!"

"Believe me or not, I did. I'm a psychic. I see, sense things. Yeah, I saw something hanging around you!"

"We-ell. Interesting, huh? What kinda something? You called it a ghost at first!" He was watching her whimsically, yet carefully, as though some tension inside him was coming to breaking point, and he seemed to be holding his breath.

She told him what she'd seen. Rob whistled, and let his breath out. "Really? Yuh think it was stalking me? Yuh reckon it shouldn't be here on our planet? Wow!"

"That's my honest impression. I do see these things, though not so frightening as this one I'm telling you about!"

He regarded her seriously, with an almost calculating expression on his face. "Are you here on your own, Janella?"

"I'm often here on my own. Can't keep away! I rowed with my

boyfriend and now he's left me, and I came here out of hurt pride, and to try and win some money to pay some expenses I owe this club!"

"Forgive me for this, but you kinda gamble, huh? Too much, if you don't mind me asking?"

Janella nodded. "I owe a lot here. I need to pay it back!" She spoke honestly before she could stop herself. Her debts were piling up.

"You're a Bretan?"

"Yeah, and you're an Amisana."

"Sure am, honey, from over the sea. Say, how'd yuh like to earn some money to help you out? Pay back what you owe?"

Janella's brilliant golden tawny eyes widened. She glanced backwards at the glowing robotic board that showed up the winning number. No more bets for her! She'd wasted her tax money. She shrugged resignedly. "What do you have in mind?"

"This strange ol' alien, would you see it again, or any more like it, apart from the two you claim yuh did see? I mean – were they ghosts, as you first claimed, or real beings?"

"Of course they were real! Both beings! That's my job! But only I saw them!"

"Swell, honey, I could really help you." Rob sounded very sincere.

There was new interest in her voice: "How?"

"I've an idea... Lady, you could be jus' the woman we're looking for. Look, if you're ready to leave, I'll get us a hover-car to take you home. Can I ride with yuh, if yuh don't mind? I'll explain what I mean on the way? We could stop off at a bar I know on the surface."

It seemed an enticing offer. Perhaps the promise of good things to come. She liked his quiet confidence and sincerity, and no alarm bells were ringing any warning. He seemed to be just a man enjoying his evening at the casino, as she had been trying to do.

She nodded. "My home is a place underwater, but, yeah, sure. Why not?"

Completely confident and with some familiarity, her new friend promptly placed his hand on her royal blue sequinned strapped shoulder and began to lead her from the casino, twisting through the crowd.

"First up, the bar I'd like to take you to is where we can talk, okay? It's a quiet place an' we won't be disturbed. Honey, I'm gonna tell you something very odd indeed an' I'm thinking, c'mon Rob, she can handle this!"

"Handle what, and what bar is this Mister? I know most around here?"

"Uh, call me Rob, right? We're going to The Dracan okay? Know it?"

"Mmm, it's a pricey joint, but lead on. I've never been inside before!"

As he led her away, a women customer standing nearby them began suspiciously to sniff the air. "I smell burning; it's coming from the roulette table!" She suddenly shouted.

All eyes shifted to the innocent-looking roulette table which was draped in a baize cloth. Another woman screamed out, whipping a fluttering hand up to her mouth in horror: "It's on fire? It's billowing out smoke from the baize top! I'm leaving!"

Rob stopped moving and glanced back at the concern and commotion. He said coolly to Janella: "'Scuse me a moment, I'm needed."

"Where are you going?"

"To troubleshoot why that table's smoking bad. Part of my job: perhaps you'd wait by the entrance door, where it's safer? I shan't be a moment!" With that he walked back, calmly bent down and lifted the table's flap and deftly, nimbly slipped underneath its folds!

The concierge hurried up to Janella, whom he knew well as she was a regular at the gaming tables.

"I've called security!" His forehead was heavily lined with worry, and his tight mock bow-tie was making him sweat badly. Janella knew the man had three other casinos in Missipania, Louisania, and Aransasia in the big country, but she didn't have the tax money to go there, too far away across the surface of the sea. "Miss Janella, do you –"

Whatever he was about to say disappeared into the ether as Rob's head popped out from under the baize table cloth. He looked grim. There was a red wire in his hand, its end tapering off to a brown and black wire entwined together.

He fluidly walked over to the concierge and spoke earnestly and softly. "Get everyone out! It's a bomb and' it's going to blow! I'm trying to stop the timer – get me a micro-spanner quick!"

The startled concierge clicked his fingers and security robots entered the casino room which was starting to thin out of those who'd been around the baize table, who had been happily wasting their money.

A micro-spanner was deftly passed into Rob McKen"s hands as he again dived beneath the table.

One of the security robots was squirting a blanket-foam over the baize cloth which was billowing smoke and smelling pungent and musty with age.

Other People at the far end of the room began to disperse sensing something was wrong. The concierge waved his arm and raised his voice. "Everyone, my apologies, please leave as quickly as you can without too much pushing and shoving. All the doors are open for you!

Leave now, please!"

Rob emerged for a second and grabbed Janella's arm. "I thought I told you to wait at the door! Quick, march!" He advised shortly. "You've got five moments only! Go! Go! Go! Sweetheart, move it!"

With everyone hurrying for the exit – except Rob – Janella hesitated, giving him a stunned, querying glance. He noticed, saying: "Don't wait for me – get out!"

"But, you –"

"Do as you're told, woman!"

Heart in mouth she turned and ran, following the concierge and his security guys as they ushered everyone to safety outside the casino.

Janella, waiting with the anxious, awed crowd outside, heard within five moments, the sound of a hover-fire machine approaching through the heavy, heated night. On this night the air was dry enough to spark a fire! On other nights the evening's surface didn't seem so bad as the intense heat of the day did!

Janella shivered slightly at her narrow escape, wishing she'd had time to collect her wrap from the cloakroom. She was worried about the man who called himself Rob McKen. Why the hell wasn't he out here by now?

It was then the casino blew up in fire and smoke with an ear-splitting bang, glass exploded from the large windows, and flames snaked through the windows and doors, flickering out into the night, eating up the stately gaming mansion...

Everyone ducked the shards of broken glass as they spewed fourth like a meteor shower. Several people were hit as they clutched their faces and shoulders, just as two hover-ambulances whisked into the drive.

The dusky crimson sky was lit up like a stage glowing red.

Concerned, Janella looked everywhere, but there was no sign of Rob.

2

It was chaotic outside as those not hurt or injured watched the holocaust and whispering among themselves, looking scared and dazed at their near escape from danger. Janella saw the concierge was talking to the firemen, gesticulating wildly and lamenting his misfortune. She was undecided what to do about Rob. Speak to the firemen she supposed, and claim a missing person who'd disappeared in the fire?

A strong hand was placed upon her arm and she spun around, her mouth open to shout out her problem to the nearest fireman. "All right, baby – let's go!"

"Oh, God, ROB, it's you! How did you get out? I thought –"

"The rear exit. Couldn't stop the bomb, but checked out the back in case anyone was still loitering around watching the shambles." He pointed nonchalantly to the blazing building as if this sort of thing happened to him everyday!

"Who are you if you know so much about trying to dismantle bombs?" Janella found her red hair was sticking to the back of her neck and she was sweating now from the heat of the night as well as the burning building.

"I'm a 'special guy' for the capital leader in our Capital City, it's like being a kind of bodyguard to him. I trained, with unusual friends, at Warren Pontina, an Amasanean Military Center. Full training given! We trained for four years solid and learned to walk through fire and smoke. Come on, let's quit this scene. I'll take you to The Drakan! 'Fraid my suit smells of fire damage! Knew I shouldn't have worn it tonight!"

She laughed, a little breathlessly. "I don't think I'll mind that! I'm glad you got out in one piece! I thought you'd been incinerated! And I don't mean by the sun either!"

"Jus' made it baby, I'm used to fast aggressive action an' dangerous decisions! Come on! I've ordered a hover taxi, it's over there, right!"

They made it to the Drakan at top speed. It was a tent-like bar room draped with overhanging ceiling sheets of white and cream.

Several hexagonal cream covered tables were dotted around the room alongside walled chair benches, whilst floating chairs were stacked in a neat pile near the curtained doorway. It was lit up in ghostly alabaster white and neon blue.

Rob paid tax money for two comfortable floating chairs, that robotically slid over to them at his bidding. He ignored the grained chair benches which looked hard and uncomfortable against this surreal bar backdrop.

The place was empty. Probably because the drinks prices were so high.

They both chose a crater of red wine from the bar list which held four x 175ml alcohol content.

Roughly, two large tumblers each. A spindly robot bought it over to them after they'd chosen from the electronic bar board. Again, Rob paid a tax chip by dropping it into a slot on the robot's front bib, a price that went through the roof and made Janella drop her jaw.

They made small talk, but Janella, bursting with curiosity asked at last: "What is this odd thing you want to tell me about, Rob?"

Rob stopped grinning from explaining about his 'special' work in the Capital, and his face grew serious.

He didn't clip his words when he said: "Those beings yuh told me about, especially the one you noticed hanging round me, I know about 'em."

"You know...? So, what gives?"

Cryptically he said: "You've struck gold, honey, an' I'm going t'tell yuh how you can get it! Do yuh comprehend me?"

Her hand was idly lying on the table. He closed his warm dry hand over hers caressingly.

She drew her hand away. "Not quite 'comprehending' you. Don't get too fresh, I'm engaged you know."

He grinned. "I like you. You speak your mind, an' not afraid to! Didn't you say you rowed with your fellah and that he'd left you all alone an' dry?"

"Why don't you tell me about these alien's? I can make my own mind up about you then!"

"Sure. But I can see you're enjoying my company – you're lovely golden eyes are sparkling!"

"Maybe they are. I like you too, but shall we get on with what we're really here for?"

"Sure, baby. I'll order some more wine. The tax pay is no object to me! Then I'll tell you what's going on an' take you home. It's pretty late now, maybe I could sleep on your sofa!"

She said, dryly: "Or in my bed by the way you're ogling me! It'll be just my luck, but I bet you're a married man!"

He squeezed her hand and grinned, saying nothing.

3

The morning came too quickly for them. Janella made coffee and cereals for Rob, and tea and toast for herself from honey bread.

Their clothes were still piled all over the hall floor in their haste to get to know each other from the night before.

Rob had kept his white crop top and trousers on for breakfast, which still smelled offensively of smoke, and she'd found her ex-boyfriend's shirt to wear, something quick and warm, that he'd left behind. Being under the sea, her flat was always chilly first thing in the morning. So it was that they chatted and flirted companionably, and she heard Rob's proposition and weird explanation with gathering interest.

Her underwater flat in Farseisia that she had shared with her boyfriend, was over a row of glassy corridor-like shops that were not in use now.

The couples row last night before she'd rushed hot-headed and tearful to the surface casino, had sent her man back to his wife for good, as she'd found when arriving home last night with Rob. A note had been left on the pseudo mantelshelf: "Goodbye you reckless bitch. Have gone back to Irena. Spend money at the casino, I don't give a damn now."

Rob had raised eyebrows when she showed him this note. All he'd said was: "Sounds a baseball bastard, sweetheart. Don't take any notice! You've got me now! I'd like to get to know you better!" He'd smirked.

"You can smirk, but you could have died in that casino! Why did those beings plant a bomb in there?"

Rob had shrugged. "Gang warfare, honey. Don't worry your pretty head about it. Let's hit the sack. I want to love you again!"

"Is that what you call it?" She'd grinned.

"So, that's it" Rob explained that morning as he crunched a wheat-induced substitute cereal she had slugged into a dish, whilst she crunched her honey toast. "You know now what we're up against sweetheart.

Think you can help?"

"Maybe. You want me to suss out these beings like I 'saw' last night and let you know about them? You want me to write about them in some kind of 'imagined' story, get it published, and help tell our planet about these beings, yeah? Well, I am a writer, but I've never done this before. I've been a scribe and artist, designing clothes for part of my life, but not writing to actually teach people things."

"The guys in high places can teach you, educate you and guide you. You're advice would be invaluable. Frankly put – it could save the planet! The news about these beings has to be sent out in a subtle way, an' you're the one to do it. I know this: you'll do a great job!"

Rob took hold of Janella's hand as she drummed it on the table. He stroked it soothingly.

"It would be a great favor for me too, honey. Last night, boy, were we good together! I'd like to see you again, an' I could show you the ropes. Never mind your ass-hole boyfriend! I work with these people I've spoken to you about. It would mean you coming to live in the capital. You could do with the break, so how about it? I have a land home in Pimlissa, it's cool an' full of cold air vents an' we could get to know each other better. That would be great for me!"

In her mind's eye, Janella recalled her trance vision of the night before. She'd envisaged a trip to the capital and to a place called Jaggard Mews! Rob went on: "Yuh could arrive by hover-rail. I'd meet you at the capital terminal an' drive you to my place. Howzat?"

"Sounds good, Rob. I like the idea... The tax lease runs out on this flat soon, and I can't afford to keep it going without Tim's tax pay. I need to move on. It's tempting. What is your place called in Pimlissa?"

"Jaggard House Mews."

Janella started. That had been in her trance impression! She was beginning to visualize the future for herself!

Rob pulled her towards him and she came willingly with a wanton smile.

"You're swell, baby! Let me tempt you to Pimlissa!"

"You're not so bad yourself!"

Now she was sitting on his lap and he caressed her body. She closed her eyes and moaned softly.

They kissed a kiss that would have exploded atoms. The spark was there, and they found it, sinking onto the kitchen floor together.

Later, relaxed and sated, he asked her again about traveling to meet him and stay in the capital..

She replied: "Yes, yes, yes! I love the idea! What about your wife though, and who are your friends?"

"Important guys. You'll see. They want to tell you stuff that's dynamite, an' to start you on the road to teaching. Incidentally, my wife left our nest for another man, sweetheart, okay?

"So you're on the rebound? Is this straight up, cause I don't just go off with anybody? Will I start soon?"

"I'm a straight guy an' it's true, an' you'll start work when we get back from our honeymoon!"

"What honeymoon? What the flame do you mean?"

"I'm gonna ask you to marry me? Will you?"

"Just after a one night-er? Are you mad, man? As you're a married man, Bretan law won't allow us to commit bigamy; we can't marry!"

"I'm as sane as you sweetheart. There's a loop-hole in Bretan law about this now; we won't be bigamists, I can assure you of that! What about it?"

Suddenly, there was a clustered engagement ring on her marriage finger, a brilliant blue lapis lazuli lying in the middle of white diamonds.

"We've only known each other since last night!"

"Hah, longer than you think, honey. I know you better than you know yourself!"

"This sounds deep. How come? You're looking at me in a very familiar way! I've never met you before last night!"

"Uh, I'll tell you about it when you join me in the capital, okay?"

"Okay. I'm content with that." She yawned, stretching out lazily, touching his shoulder. "I'm too tired to take in any more now. Let's take a sexy shower together, get dressed properly and go up to the surface for a lovely walk in the nearest park!"

"Hope I can borrow some of your ex's clothes? I'll look cranky wearing my once white top crop and suit trousers! They stink!"

"I'll find you something, Rob, you're about the same height and waist as Tim. It's a pleasure having you here! I'm glad I met you!"

"Sure, same here, sweetheart!"

As they walked in the surface park, which was near their underwater cave exit, hand-in-hand, Rob kept his eyes open – just in case anyone was following them. He knew the casino bomb had not been an accident, but a planted incident that may or may not relate to him and his danger-job.

4

Their romance took off. The only fly in the ointment was Rob's ex-wife, whom he readily admitted he still adored, who lived in Amisana. She was the mother of his five young children ranging from five to fourteen years old, and Janella guessed, still had claims on Rob's heart through their past links and their children, even though, his wife Estellene, had left their marital home for another man fifteen years younger than her.

Just a month after Janella had met Rob and they were making love waves and joyous plans to live in the capital and see her new home, Janella received a call on her hand-held mobile board.

Faintly, a woman's voice said: "It's Estellene McKen calling you, Janella."

The woman's name flashed to confirm her status, and with proof of who she really was.

This was a turn-up! What did Estellene McKen want with her?

"Hallo, are you Rob's wife?"

"I've confirmed it with my picture, yes." Estellene's voice sounded prim with a Southern Amisean drawl. She had looked ill in the picture that had flashed up on Janella's board; a horsey face with long narrow cheekbones and puffy under-eyes that looked glazed with pain. Her head had been lying on a pillow and her brownish hair looked awry as if something had happened to her.

Something also in Estellene's voice alerted Janella to close her eyes to enter a trance state. She saw and sensed a disturbing thing...

Janella felt Estellene's pain, as Rob's wife spoke faintly now. "I've had a car smash... Am in the ambulance with a broken pelvis. Can you tell Rob to come home? I need him by my side, please, tell him that."

Janella's trance took her to the ambulance Estellene was in. She saw at once the woman was telling the truth. As she watched her trance play out, she noticed the two paramedics that were administering first aid to her. Then, it seemed, another figure had appeared there.

To her horror, she saw the same type of being sidling away that had appeared to be beside Rob on the night she'd met him at the casino! This strange animal-like creature looked slightly shorter and different to the one she'd seen before!

What was it doing watching Estellene McKen? Had it been with her in her car? Janella couldn't be sure. She narrowed her eyes and came out of trance, wondering whether she should tell Rob this. She decided he had enough worries, but, damn! Where she was concerned, it might mean Rob would have to go home! Estellene had a hold on him now: he might not return to her she thought remorsefully, but said as professionally as she could:

"Don't worry: I'll call Rob now, Estellene."

There was no answer on the other end; Estellene had fainted.

When she contacted Rob, his face on the board looked distraught. "God-damn it! Is it serious? Is she hurt bad?"

"She's broken her pelvis. She'll be in hospital for about a month. Obviously you'll have to go back to her. She said she needs you!"

"Hh-mm. It's a moot point... Fuck! Just as we were getting on so mighty fine!"

"It bothers me.... You might not come back if you return to her."

"'Course I will – you're giving me a queer look, don't tell me you're jealous of Estellene!"

"I don't want to lose you! Do you really have to go? Can't you stay here with me?"

"She's asked for me, she IS my ex-wife whom I've parted from. I'm duty-bound to go back. Our kids will want me to."

Janella made a face and groaned. "I couldn't bear it if you left me now!"

Hard anger suddenly made Rob's voice sound rough. "Don't use emotional blackmail on me, honey, I have to return!"

It was the first time she'd encountered his stern voice, and it shook her. His eyes and face wore a determined, stubborn look that warned her to back off. Seeing her stricken expression he produced a tight, belated smile on her call screen that didn't reach his eyes.

"Trust me! I promise you, got to because there's my job at Worpminster to consider. I ain't gonna leave that to the mutts who work there to take over from me!"

"You're right; I wasn't thinking straight. Estellene's call jarred me, that's all."

"It's jarred me, too. How'd the silly bitch do it?"

"She swerved off the highway."

"So my car I left her with is a right-off!"

"Never mind your stupid car! She's been hurt! She'll need your sympathy, Rob, which is more than your giving me! Don't be so hard! This must really have rattled you for you to get so riled!"

"I don't like what's happened, is all, and she is my ex-wife! That car was expensive!"

"Then you'd better leave this wire and go get off to her if that's how you feel!"

Her snappiness brought him to his senses abruptly.

"Aw – sorry! I didn't mean to hurt your feelings, honey. Shouldn't take it out on you! I worry about all the members of my past family, I was a family man!"

"I know that! But don't blame me for what's happened!"

"My apologies, sweetheart, thanks for telling me this."

Thank God for that! You're voice is sincere again! Oh, I do love you, Rob!"

"I love you, too. It's jus' a hiccup in our plans, doll. I'll return, okay?"

"How long will you be gone?"

"Ah, mebbe two weeks, don't know. Sit tight and wait for me, honey – promise?"

"I'll wait for you 'till the world stops turning! Sorry if I howled at you!" She lowered her lips to kiss the call board and left him smiling at her passion. He blew an airy kiss back before her screen blanked out.

5

Janella's life went blank knowing Rob had gone off to be with Estellene in Amisana.

A hollow hole torn in a page would have described how she felt without Rob, even though he called her twice a day from his own big country.

She learned Estellene wasn't doing too badly and that Rob would join her in Farseisia again within two weeks.

She began to strike off the days on her mobile board as they happened. Time seemed to move slowly for her. She missed his loving presence, his laconic, dry humor, and his sexual advances – which were virile and wholesome!

Yet within three days she'd had a wonderful surprise that stunned her deeply because it was so unexpected.

Her mobile board trilled its music and she answered eagerly, thinking it might be Rob. "Yes, hallo?"

No picture came up. A strange, hearty Amisanean male voice spoke richly and simply: "Rob's on his way, sweetheart – just thought you'd like to know!" And her line went dead. She couldn't bring any details back and her caller had blocked her finding out who he was!

Puzzled, she tried trance, to see what was happening, but nothing came up.

It worried her; was Rob okay?

As she stood, frowning over this weird contact, a pair of warm, stale-sweat, travel stained hands closed over her unsuspecting eyes, momentarily startling her.

"H'ya honey, have you missed me!"

It was Rob's voice, and she could now smell a whiff of his expensive aftershave which hadn't masked the smell of his hands. She felt suddenly flooded with joy, and found her own tone, swinging around freely to face him: "I – oh – I don't believe this! It's so good to see you again! Where the hell did you spring from? I wasn't expecting you for ages! It's only been four days since you left, Rob!"

Laughing, he cuddled her, crushing her to him. "Surprised,

sweetheart?"

"Oh, yes you devil! I've missed you so much! How come you're back so early? Is your wife – has something hap –?"

"Shh-shh, nothing bad, angel. She's on the mend. I've returned as promised, 'cause I couldn't stay away from you another day! You're my life now!"

"Oh Rob, I do so love you!" She flung her arms around him, her voice and eyes throbbing with passion.

They made love in the kitchen again, kicking off clothes frantically, uncaring of the coolness of the floor as they sank down on it, kissing and cuddling like boxing kangaroos let loose from their cages.

. . . .

By mid-Septer calendar month Janella was out of the flat in Farseisia, ready to start her new life on Deitto's surface in Capital City, and was already being paid in tax chips, which helped her refund her debts to her favorite fire-destroyed casino, which was going to move to a new location she heard.

True to his word Rob picked her up in his brand new design hover-Porsche at the nearest capital hop-rail station, and flew her to his old-fashioned mews home in Pimlissa, a suburb of the Capital City.

The capital teemed with burning rays of Septer sun, and a blanket of dust lay over the city making the sky look fawn-hazy. There were busy people walking by and hover-vehicles flying low everywhere.

Rob kissed her full-on and hoisted her baggage into his hover-machine, panting a little in the dry heat. As they lifted off he said to her: "Some unusual friends of mine are dying to meet you babe. I'll show you around my home, we'll have salladio nicoise, then I'll hover towards Worpminster, where you know I work for our capital leader. It's the capital's hub, okay?"

"Fine, Rob. Who are your friends?"

"Important guys, as I say – unusual guys. You'll see. They'll want to tell you things"

"Unusual friends, you keep stressing that word! In what way?"

"You could say my friends have a 'hidden' agenda is the best way to explain it..."

"I don't understand."

"You will. You'll like them, their great guys! Think I told you, we were all trained at Warren Pontina Military Academy."

"Yes, you did. Sounds good. Will I start straight away on this new writing stories job?"

"Yeah, after our honeymoon on board the Silver Star. We'll get married on her."

"Married! Aren't you rushing along a bit? I really need to know who your friends are first."

"Listen, hon, I was going to explain after we'd had our food. Because you're asking now – my friends know your powers, an' we've been following your progress for some time. It was no accident I was at that casino in July. I followed you there to introduce myself to you!"

"On purpose, Rob? What's going on? You keep dropping bombshells on me! Why are you all so interested in me?"

"Don't get jiggered. Sit still sweetheart. I have to tell you, you've been leading a double life without knowing it. An' that's why my friends all know you. So do I. It's a long story. Look, we're here outside the mews now – welcome home Janella! We'll have a drink an' I'll tell you a story yuh just won't believe!"

Where he'd stopped the hover-Porsche she noticed the slabbed pavement with deep sunken drain covers. Rob said proudly: "These slabs date back to the late eighteen hundreds."

"Really? That long ago, how quaint! You have a lovely home, Rob."

"Sure have, baby, an' it's all yours as well! Shall I carry you in like your 'quaint' old custom asks?"

"We're not married yet!"

"But we will be honey. I have plans for you!"

He carried her into his mews home dating back to the 21st Century, and the old pavement slabs which dated beyond that. Around the porch-way door were hung two actual gleaming metallic carriage lamps of yesteryear.

She entered her new home with a song in her heart.

6

After taking her baggage up to their bedroom, Rob made saladio nicoisse with an egg on top, and poured a beer for him and wine for Janella. Then he explained to a dumbstruck Janella what she needed to know.

She was shaking her head, biting her lip. "Rob – I can't believe this! It sounds bizarre! How could Worpminster make use of my psychic abilities without me knowing? You say I've been doing two jobs all my life, that I have some kind of double identity? I have a doppelganger?"

"We've used your mental imaginary, sweetheart. Mind matters. We've brought this into the open for a reason you'll one-day suss out. We need you now, to help the world with your abilities. You'll have my name and a completely different life. An I want to be with you and help you change that, honey. I mean this, I'm sincere, and love you deeply – let's go upstairs an' I'll show you the view from the top! The bed's been made apple-pie ready for us, right here, right now!"

"You seriously think I'm going to bed with you now?"

"Why not? I can't wait to prove how much I love you!"

"I'm sure you can't, lover! You'll need to tell me more about this job I'm supposed to be doing for the government, presumably in your bed, I guess!"

Upstairs, the view from the old mews was splendid. She could see people and the traffic sprawling around Pimlissa. Further away in the looming fawn-haze there were green parks, rusty-roofed houses and subtle hills and valleys in the distance, where lay domed and turreted skyscrapers.

"This might be a suburb of the capital but we do have some greenery!" Rob joked. He pulled her onto the old-fashioned king-size bed and plucked down her strapless top, kissing her puckering breasts...

7

The capital leader Peter Hopgood-Royce, pushed back his cherry-wood floating chair and rose quickly, holding his hand out to Janella, whilst brushing lunch crumbs from his suit.

She and Rob had been ushered into the Oval room by the CL's under-secretary, a thin reed of a man also named Peter, who fussed about pushing the floating cherry-wood chairs over for Janella and Rob to sit in.

Outside his oval-shaped and latticed window she could hear the hover hum of the City. The window was open, letting in the hot sunlight. Cool air blasters were churning non-stop in the background. There was the faint smell of food in the room.

Hopwood-Royce beamed in delight at her.

"Welcome m'dear. Very pleased to meet you at last!" His handshake was pudgy, warm and dry.

Having shaken hands they all resumed their seats. There was a pleasant ambiance in this large room with its old Indian carpet, large shiny desk and floating, yet classic polished chairs.

Janella relaxed as the whiskey and sherry in large oval cut-glass decanters were handed around discreetly by the CL's male secretary without spilling a drop of alcohol.

The sherry offered was excellent, deeply red, and beefy-sweet. After some admiring pleasantries, Hopwood-Royce reached his business level and cleared his throat in preparation of what he knew he must now tell her. She sipped with interest as he outlined his plans for her.

"Janella, you've come a long way in your psychic development now and I believe the time has come to be frank with you. We need your help again."

"Because of the Alligator being I saw in my trance that you, Rob, and the other operatives, Rob's unusual friends, know about?"

"Precisely."

"It's been claimed by Rob here that I've led a double life!"

"Very true. You have been the perfect psychic model for us for some years now. Sorry you weren't told."

"I would have liked to have known about it!"

"We had to pick the right time to tell you of your activities, which you would not have believed possible unless you'd seen our film archives of you!"

"I'd certainly like to see those! But how did you manage to do it without me knowing?"

Hopgood-Royce smiled sweetly. "You did it, by astral walking in the night, going to places that needed help, in an 'invisible' state. Your higher self was signed up to me almost instantly, because there aren't many Deittonean females like you about! I've been capital leader here for many years, and I made your astral self sign an agreement to help us! You've done so relentlessly and we all know you, so there's not need to stand on ceremony with me!"

"But why wasn't I aware of this myself! Somehow, a mirror image of me has been used without my knowledge! No wonder I've felt so tired sometimes, if my higher self did all this stuff you've mentioned! And, having met you now, I have a vague recollection of a dream which I had years ago and we were both in it. It was as if I was speaking to you and listening to your decisions, as if you were making your mind up about me. We reached some kind of agreement!"

"You are probably right! Your dream may have been a hundred percent real! It takes years for the astral self to enter your consciousness. When it does, you 'wake-up' – as you are already now finding out!"

"So...what have I done to help out?"

"We'll show you when I authorize the archive films removal from their files. Be content to wait until then, Janella."

"Now you want me to help you further, as myself?"

"Correct. You are wise enough, strong enough, and powerful enough to do so. The Lize-nards as we call them, are beings that plan an overrun of our planet. You have already been told about that.

For helping us now I can give you remuneration on a large scale, to make up for any past losses.

"So, that's the situation. Think you'll like my generous offer?" He named a price that raised Janella's eyebrows.

"It sounds fair and just: you want me to use my psychic gifts and discreetly spread the word of this menace that is bothering our world by creative writing. But I'll tell you and Rob something else now: Rob, remember when Estellene had her accident?"

"As if I could forget. What's this to do with her?"

"I went into trance and saw her in the hover-ambulance with two medics. I also saw one of these menaces you've been on about. I believe it knows I saw it. The being was crowding around Estellene's cot whilst the medics applied first aid. They didn't see it, but I did, in my mind's eye!

It seemed to be watching her pain and enjoying it. I believe it may have caused her accident, because it may have appeared and showed itself to her, causing her to swerve off the road like she did!"

Hopgood-Royce stood up abruptly. "Do you realize what you are saying Janella? By God, she might be right!"

Rob stood up too. "Janella, you've pulled this out of the hat, surprising me like that! Are you saying Estellene may be in danger – or, was in danger from this unholy alien being!"

Janella nodded.

"I'd better go warn her! It could be stalking her like Janella saw it stalking me!" Rob was halfway to the door when the CL called out: "Rob – wait! I'll get President Osmund in Amisana to send his troopers to your, ahem, ex-wife. No need to take alarm yet, we'll keep it all in hand. Come back and sit down. You're with Janella now, remember!"

"How can I cool my heels when my ex may be in danger! And possibly, my kids?" Rob looked worried and angry.

"I might be wrong, Rob. Don't jump the gun yet. Peter's right; we'll have to wait and see." Janella caught his hand as he swung past her in a dramatic vexed movement. "I think you must still think a lot of her."

Rob reddened. "So would you after eighteen years of marriage!" He retorted.

Janella dropped her hand. It was the answer she'd suspected; it sounded like Rob still loved his wife above her. She'd heard the loyalty in his voice. She lowered her eyes, a jagged tear forming, and quickly, before either man could see, brushed it angrily away. It made her say to Hopgood-Royce: "I'm not happy you've used my double 'me' before without my knowing!"

"You will be amply rewarded for past endeavors, m'dear. I've explained why dear lady. I'm sure you'll agree we've thought of everything for you. My profuse apologies for not telling you before and ask your forgiveness now." He held out his hand winsomely with a boyish smile. He was so charismatic!

After a moment's hesitation she nodded and shook his hand again lightly.

Rob and Hopgood-Royce looked pleased at her compliance. They had both settled back in their chairs, although Rob kept flashing a look at the old-fashioned ticking clock on the wall in some exasperation.

Hopgood-Royce stood with a flourish. "Very, very regretfully, I have a meeting to attend, but we'll be in touch after your honeymoon, and I congratulate you both and wish you every success for the future."

"Thank you."

"One other thing; there is a Gala Ball I'd like you to attend after you both get back from abroad. The King will be there and I'll be proud to introduce you to him. He is looking forward to meeting you! I must say, Rob is a very lucky man to have found such a charmer as you! Don't worry about a thing you two. We'll keep it sewn up for now, right? And Rob, I will keep an eye on Estellene's welfare, and your children, okay man? You must worry about Janella now! You've been warned!" There was a meaningful look in Peter Hopgood-Royce's blue eyes.

"Sure, boss." Rob nodded, but said it tongue in cheek, swallowing any others words he'd wished to add as carefully as his rugged countenance would let him

8

They packed for their cruise upon their liner, The Silver Star, which floated to several countries on the planet Deitto, but finally docked in a holding bay at Bandivarra, a Barissean-type holiday island.

It was a beautiful place of sea winds and soft clouds floating in a rainbow sky. Sharp, jagged shore line rocks were softened by dangling seaweed as the warm Barissean tide rose and cropped them with rusty-white waves, and they reflected the amazing sunset of indigo blue, scarlet red, fluorescent mossy green, and gray tones.

Their wedding that morning on the ship had been a quiet affair, with an aging, fatherly ship's pastor joining them in matrimony without any guests being present. Janella had worn a sea-green gown and her groom an all-in-one white suit.

Their hilltop home overlooking the sparkling Deitto Sea that separated them from Janella's country was as white-washed and fresh as the private beach below them, glowing like frozen ice-chips from the late evening sun. In contrast, the air was heavy, lurid and very warm.

Dark, gnarled, misshapen trees smudged the distant shoreline. Their 'villa' behind them was a double-floored 'open-aired' home on two split-levels, one block above the other, and was smart and spacious.

Janella stood marveling at the view, long hair blowing softly in the wind. Rob crept up behind her, his favorite approach, and placed his hands around her waist, kissing smoothly all over her tanned shoulder.

She giggled and said: "It's lovely here, it's paradise! So-o-o romantic!"

"Great, honey, sure!" He fondled her hair and produced some sun-lotion.

"Mrs McKen-Black, I care about that lovely back. Don't get burnt, even if the sun is going down! I'll put some stuff on."

She closed her eyes in ecstasy at his sensual touch. Then her world clouded over and she was back in trance. She found she was staring at something. She stiffened in alarm.

"What's wrong?" He stopped rubbing after sun lotion on her bare back.

"I'm seeing things... Rob, it's that same creature come back that I told you about, the being I saw at the casino the night I met you!"

"Hell – where, honey!"

"In front of me right now."

"I can't darn-well see it! Stand behind me for pete's sake, Janella – don't step over to it!"

"Wait! It's talking in a strange dialect, eons old. I might be able to understand it."

"Don't move! I'll get my gun!"

"No. No! I sense this one is friendly. Stay by me. Don't use any weapons on it. It needs love, not violence. Let me talk to it... Hi! Why are you here, following us around? What do you want?"

Unheard, yet sensed, words flowed into her mind from the being before her, talking in her own dialect.

And she realised she hadn't been told all the truth yet. It cut right through her...

"Child of the dark, I am as black as Hades, call me by many names, I will whisper words and you will understand me. When this enters your consciousness you will translate what I say to you in your mind. This information that I give you readily relates from the beginning of your Planet Deitto, which us beings knew as Planet Danek in the old times.

You can see me. I and many others exist here on Deitto now. Your people have allowed us entry and we have given them creative ideas to brighten up Deitto, creating love and happiness. But there is a catch...

Now, sweep your inner psychic eye to mine, and your truth of yourself will be foretold through Deitto's centuries of time. Listen well...

Untold years have passed. You have wandered through time as Deitto's Guardian. You are its Avatar and wise woman and you have the sight. Believe this to be true. You have been awakened to learn this. You are part of the whole, we are all one cohesive presence in this world."

"How do you mean, we are all one?" Janella realized she'd asked this in her mind, and this being had translated her thought.

"You will understand this better when you're psychic sense becomes one with others on this planet. You are moving towards your destiny and your inner knowledge of self. When you understand this, everyone else will too."

Now, listen to me, there are those like me upon your planet who have multiplied through bonding with Deitto's females, creating hybrid children. These beings, like me, are outlander's from another world who have no children to keep their planet open to survival. They have been here millions of years, 6.5 billion years ago to be precise. We owned this planet before you landed here and colonized it for yourselves. We came back here 40 years ago, and were even visiting this planet before then, for our planet was dying. There were only a handful of us on Deitto when we started, now the hybrid children birthed here today, using Deittonean females, will turn this into thousands...

You are called to use your sight to help people who know we are in your world and spread word of it. You must speak of love as true love, which must be accepted by Deittoneans and hybrid beings as well.

Your visions and higher contacts you make when you return to the land capital of Deitto with your husband will help you.

These beings who look like me, will only show up under a certain light, invisible to the eyes of most Deittoneans, which is why there is no panic yet. I foretell, a special machine or instrument, or psychedelic drug will be used in the future to show these beings up, and you will 'see' them and who they are attached to.

Janella mind-thought back to the creature standing placidly before her. "Attached to? Explain what you mean?"

"We can 'latch on' to top people and bend them to our rules and make them obey us. But I do not do that. I was trying to 'latch on' to Rob McKen in the casino that night, to speak to him and warn him further of our plans. But you came in and sensed me in your trance, and I had to disappear. Now I know you work with him and are married to him, I can approach you."

"Did you know I also saw another being like you, who planted a bomb there!"

"I knew that. It was why I wanted to speak to your husband."

"Let's get this straight: you were trying to help him, knowing he works for the Government, is that it?"

"You are astute, yes."

"You're a good guy?"

"I have said so, yes. Now, trust me. I know you from old. I am a friend – even if I am one of them. That is enough for you to know now. The man you married and those top men you have already spoken to have not told you all yet. Farewell beauty. I will contact again soon."

Stunned at all this information, Janella spoke back in her mind: "Do you mean those I met in the capital before this honeymoon started?"

"Yes. Your new husband is not what he seems!"

"What are you trying to say?"

A cryptic answer came back.

"You will find out. I am leaving now."

"Wait – wait! The casino bomb! You say that was nothing to do with you?"

"Not me, no, but they were my kind, and they are evil, with intent to control your planet. Despite what we started to do for you at the beginning, this is their final, terrible plan. It is not for your planet, but for them..."

"I'm losing you! Come back!"

Her trance disintegrated. She was left staring at the stunning sea view, her mind in a whirl of thoughts too bizarre to believe!

Rob raced up with his slug gun and she stared at it in awe. "I didn't know you had that!"

"Can't be too careful, honey."

"There's nothing to slug at – its gone!"

"Are you okay, did it say anything to you?"

"I'm shaken, but okay... No, it said nothing! Too scared of me, I think! Any case, I didn't understand it even if it did say anything!" She wondered why she lied. Somehow, this strange half-beast of a being had blown her world in two, and left her doubtful of those she spoke to in the present – including Rob, who she loved with all her heart at the moment.

Later that night, when they went for a midnight swim and made love on the beach, her mind was on other things... And torn, she slept restlessly. Mainly, wondering who she could really trust.

It felt like the honeymoon was over. She said to herself, "Oh, shit, I feel older than Rob now! Thanks to that cursed bogey-being who's got a face like an alligator's! Why did he come into my life now, just when things were going right for me?"

9

Back in Bretan again and Rob and Janella returned to their mews home in Pimlissa. Rob was called into work straight away, leaving Janella to unpack and wash their holiday clothes, which she began attending to with a will-do attitude and enthusiasm, despite the dragging heat of the day.

She entered their shared, large sunny bedroom intent on hanging one of her evening dresses away.

It was sweltering in the bedroom with only one top window open. She made to move towards a built-in wardrobe that sensed her presence and opened it's sliding door for her, but found she couldn't move another step for some reason, no matter how much she tried!

It was like coming into contact with an invisible glass door! She spread her arms out to 'feel' around the edges, searching for an outlet, then froze, mute and transfixed, suddenly feeling a man's arms crushing her shoulders inwards, whilst hard lips seized her mouth in a fever-gripping kiss!

What the hell was this?

Something was said, but she didn't hear what it was.

Alarmed, she tried to step back, but found her head crushed to a manly chest complete with a heart beat that she could feel and hear, throbbing soundly beneath her left ear. Whoever, whatever it was seemed to be wearing some kind of short-sleeved button shirt – although she couldn't see it, she could feel it!

She couldn't cry out. The demanding kiss went on and on, and her heart beat a fast tattoo alongside this unknown assailant's even breathing. What the flame was happening? Was this some kind of mind hallucination she was experiencing because of the heat? Or had she gone into a different type of trance?

A voice spoke in her head much like the Voldan's had done, entering her consciousness without interpretation. It was Amisanean, vibrant, strong, and very friendly!

"Hi Janella, welcome to Pimlissa. We've been waiting for you, baby. I'm sure glad to meet you at last, in person!"

She managed to peel her lips away, blinking rapidly to clear her eyes, still held in this unseen embrace, as if in some kind of time-lock.

"Who the hell are you? I can't see you!"

"We're Rob's 'unusual' friends, honey. We're all guys who've trained at Warren Pontena Military Academy in Amisana. We trained in a four year commissioning program an' received academic, military, physical and character instructions from our UMSA staff. We even did a 6 weeks introduction to learn how to walk through fire and smoke. It blew our minds, babe!"

"You are blowing mine! I've heard this before somewhere... Whose 'we', some kind of ex-cadets?"

"There are five of us here, in your bedroom. Now don't scream; we're not here to frighten you, lady. We're Rob's friends as said, an' he's gotta whole big surprise for yuh!"

"What surprise? This is so bizarre! Why am I going daft talking to thin air? Why can't I see you all? It's frightening me – not seeing anyone!"

"Sorry about that, I'll explain in a moment... First off, I know it's a lot to take in Janella, but listen to me; I'm Tom Wilson; I'm Rob's best pal... Second, here is Clay Coleby – who can't wait to say his piece!"

There was a slight shift of dry air as Tom moved from her side and made way for Clay.

Another pair of unseen hands were placed on her shoulders. A steady kiss again clamped her mouth shut. "Hi honey. I'm Clay Coleby from Canterey country, close to the border of Amisana."

"Mmm mmm mmm! I don't believe this! What's going on? Get the hell off me! I, I'll fight you!"

"Don't be alarmed. We're on the level, sweetheart. Let me shake your hand to show we mean you no harm." Invisibly, 'Clay' put his hand in hers and shook it. His fingers were warm and long and supple. His handshake firm, strong, and strangely comforting. "How do you do?"

Dazed, but somewhat mollified, she replied: "This is weird...talking to nothing, yet I feel you kiss me and shake my hand. I even feel the buttoned shirt Tom is wearing!"

"Because you're a sensitive psychic lady, that's why!"

"Look, I'm rattled, are you ghost friends of Rob? I could understand that, I think!"

She thought she sensed a grin on their faces, but wasn't sure. Her imagination was working overtime, and her heartbeat sped with it!

Tom spoke kindly to her, intuitively sensing she was still suspicious of them.

"It's Tom, sweetheart. We're not ghosts, we're as human as you are, just invisible to you at the moment. You'll see us one day soon. Now, meet Brett Kerr." Tom continued.

"Hi, Skipper!" Brett's voice sounded twangy and down-to-earth. He pumped her hand hard. There followed a kiss on her cheek and one on her mouth, very long and subtle. "I'm from the land of upside-downers – Ausina Country!"

Surprised, she exclaimed: "You're an Ausina? My adopted uncle used to call me Skipper when we were on his boat, over in your country! How do you know what he used to call me? He's dead now!"

Tom said: "We know everything about you. We've known you as long as Rob has, although he's not a 'special invisible agent' like us."

"But, like, I haven't long met Rob! I don't get this, how come? I don't know any of you, or remember your names in my life!"

"Later, we'll explain. Now, meet Todd Rogers– he's an Amisana military artist!"

Todd joyfully kissed her long and hard on the lips too, holding her tightly as if he really knew her intimately! She sussed he had long hair, for the tendrils rippled across her face. She was astonished, as she struggled to catch her breath from all this kissing.

"And I'm Ben Swift. It's great meeting you again, lovely! I'm Breton." A Bretonean voice, firm, and throbbing with a kind of excitement in his tone. Another smooch of a kiss.

She was suddenly aware she was getting another signal from someone on her right hand side. It seemed familiar, and she looked around quickly thinking to 'see' who this familiar being was who seemed to have some affluence over her which she'd sensed immediately she'd come into the bedroom. There seemed to be a man here with a strong personality. He was oozing charm and sensual warmth, as if the sun-nova shone every day on him.

"Hi, baby," the voice was smooth, masculine, confident, and sure of itself and its welcome.

She was held lovingly in the crook of his arm as he kissed her smoothly and sexily, lips, tongue, the entire assemblage. Wow!

"Remember me, honey? I'm Red McBride. Like Ben jus' said it's one hell of a swell to meet you again!" Another Amisana she assumed, by his warm, comforting, hearty welcoming tone.

"Look – explain. I must be going mad! You're obviously here, unseen. But why? What kind of magic is this?"

Tom answered her question. He seemed the most caring and helpful one. "We're astral walkers, baby. You can do this too. We split from the atom of our main selves an' fly anywhere we want. You've done this when you worked for Deitto's central office board before, at Capital City

– although you didn't know it. Now their asking you to do it again. We work with Rob as invisible operatives and help the capital leader. Do you comprehend now?"

Daylight flashed in her mind. "The capital stole my second body and used me for other purposes! Is that how it was done? You wait 'till I speak to Peter Hopgood-Royce! He owes me, big-time for this fantastic fantasizing!"

Tom spoke again. "It's all true about you and us, honey, and Rob doesn't mind us visiting you in this way."

"How do you mean? More revelations?"

Tom stood in front of her and regarded her lovingly, although she couldn't see him!

"As said, we've known you for years, sweetheart. We'll explain in the pick-up jet that's coming here to take us all away soon."

"What pick-up jet?"

Ben's Bretonean voice answered her: "Rob's surprise, darling. We're all going to one of Deitto's docking bays to meet him there."

There was a honking noise out in the street.

Tom continued: "There's no need to unpack. Get your baggage and we'll go!"

"Er, look, friends you might be, of his, but I need to confirm this. Also, how is it you all seem to know me so intimately!"

She felt Tom take hold of her arm. "Explanations on the way. Call Rob – he's expecting it. He knew we were coming here to make your acquaintance this morning. Let's go baby! You're safe with us!"

"He didn't tell me about expecting any call from me!"

"Huh, that's Rob, he loves surprises! Are you ready?"

10

On the pick-up jet, Janella called Rob on her private line.

"Rob, what's going on? I'm er, with your friends in a pick-up jet bound for the docking station. Can you confirm this...unusual meeting and suspenseful surprise they've said you planned for me, I'm still puzzled?"

"Sure, honey. It's true. Hope what I planned didn't faze yuh too much! I'm already at the docks, waiting for you!"

"What's happening?"

"Top orders. We're having another holiday break – it's special, sweetheart. Glad you've met the boys. They are great guys and you know them well!"

"So they say. I don't get it."

"You will, lovely. I'll explain when you see me. We've time for a tea-break before the ship leaves."

"What are you on about? What ship?"

"Uh, time for me to go. The guy's will look after you. See you soon honey!"

11

When she arrived at the shipping bay, to all extents and circumstances on her own, although she was aware that 'Tom' was holding her hand, Janella spied Rob waiting for her.

He was standing outside a small eating house attached to the bays. It had an open glowing type of archway door in blaring neon-yellow tones, and with polished green and black-lit up grid-lines on the floor, and yellow booths inside.

The holding bays to her right were dark and shadowed, but each cruise ship stood out in gleaming white like ghostly sentinels on guard, ready to shift and float out to the sea from their neon-blue lit opened bay hanger doors.

She ran up to him and he whisked her off her feet with strong arms and kissed her soundly.

"Oh, Rob! I thought you'd be at work by now!"

"Hi sweetheart. You've met the boys? Good. We've got half hour to spare before we depart, let's have some food in here." He shook imaginary hands with 'the guys', seeming to 'see' them more than she could, and ushered her into the eating house, which was empty of customers.

With no one else in there the party had the place to themselves. Which was a good thing: Janella had thought Rob looked funny shaking hands in thin air to invisible men that no one else could see. Tom began to explain things to Janella as she and Rob sipped cool beverages and munched iced banana rolls.

When Tom had finished his explanation Janella looked ruffled. Rob gripped her hand tightly, trying to explain further what Tom had spoken about.

"You see sweetheart, that's why you are really needed here, and why you're with us now."

"Look, I didn't know I was living a double life, and now you all tell me I'm some kind of love siren, and you've all seemed to 'share' me in the past! I just can't believe it! And I didn't know! Everything's coming to light! Why have I been told now – Does that make me some kind of whore?"

Rob squeezed her hand, which she quickly snatched back. "Don't feel bad about it. We've taken care of you; you're our world an' we can't do without you."

"But, I don't get it. If I'm some kind of scarlet woman or 'goddess' to you men, why wake me up now, to the situation that's happening here?"

"The top guys need you to suss out the Lize-nard situation you've already been told about."

"Okay, I'm trying to come round to it, but why are we all here, and why can't I see your friends? I can only feel and hear them! It's a double shock to learn of leading a double life as well as being some kind of tart! It sounds like I've been working all my life! You all make me feel older than I look!"

Rob genuinely smiled at her and squeezed her hand. "You've been with us ever since you were thirteen, sweetheart!"

"I-I find this so hard to take in! I just didn't know my other half was being used like that!"

She felt Tom take hold of her hand now and she looked in the direction she thought he was sitting.

Tom's voice sounded in her ear: "You will see us soon, and you have worked all your life. That's why we know you so well. We've grown up with you!"

"How could you? We've all been living miles apart. You certainly didn't attend my school when I was thirteen!"

Tom replied: "We all flew to you, baby, at various times. Can you imagine that?"

"Ah, you've lost me! Did you say flew?"

"Sure. Even when young we could do this; so could you!"

"I'm gob smacked – I really do not know what to say! Are we talking astral flying?"

"Sure am! Our higher selves separate and fly to your call!"

"But I wasn't aware of 'calling' you!"

Rob again took her hand and held it tightly. He grinned adoringly at her.

"Like it or not, you're our magnetic angel, an' we stick to you! The laws of attraction is various in many guises! In answer to your first question, the top guys have another surprise gift for us – we're going on an interplanetary trip around Deitto, again on the Silver Star, hence meeting at this shipping bay. They've given you another present! How do yuh like that?"

"With you, Rob?"

"With all of us! We're sharing you, honey."

"The voyage sounds great, not sure about all this sharing! I had no idea I was such a strumpet!"

"You're not. Don't think badly of yourself; your our girl – in our little circle, sweetheart. Remember that! We won't tire you out too much! We'll all cuddle you an' give you plenty of kisses!"

"Thanks, no heavy petting, or man-handling I assume! But didn't the Capital Leader, Peter, say something about attending a Gala Ball soon? I'll be whacked out by then!"

"Not till the end of the month, sweetheart. Don't let that worry you; you'll be very honored by those invited to the ball. Least-ways, we'll be back at Pimlissa by then!"

"Then how will you all 'share me'? I haven't said I like the idea yet?"

"You will; we'll treat you like a lady because we all love you within our small circle of seven. Why feel so bad about it?"

"Because I'll have too many boyfriends! It'll make me feel – I don't know – used, I suppose!"

"We all love you. Isn't that enough?

"Yeah, but it makes me feel so weird, being put on some damn goddess-like pedestal, as if I'm some famous lady!"

"Jan, you are, to us, you jus' don't see how you fit in yet, but you will, sweetheart, I promise you!"

"But –"

"Jus' concentrate on us. We'll all look after you in our own ways and, boy, do I have some plans for you! That's true, isn't it fellah's?"

Red must have stood up. From the opposite side of the table, he leaned over and planted a kiss on Janella's cheek. She could feel the dynamics of him exuding from his pores. He was such a powerful presence! "Janella, baby, I welcome you back. We all do!"

One by one, Rob, Tom, Brett, Todd, Clay and Ben all stood, leaned over and planted a kiss on her cheek and one on her mouth.

Rob said: "Go for it honey!"

Tom squeezed her hand. "I second that. Don't worry; we'll help you settle in with us!"

Brett said: "Okay Skipper, you're one of us now!"

Ben said heartily: "Welcome back, darling!"

Todd hugged her, saying: "Great to have you here in person now! We've really looked forward to this moment!"

And tall Clay said practically: "Yeah, this is great, I second that! You're with us big boys now! C'mon, we're going to miss the ship if we stay here too long! Ready to roll, honey?"

"Seems I'm outnumbered!" Entering into the spirit of the occasion, Janella added: "Okay, guys, I'm with you!. Red, gimme your hand!" She sought for and found Red's hand and entwined her left hand through Rob's right arm. "Okay guys, let's go! Just remember to treat me right; I'm still bemused!"

12

Their second trip was eventful. They had the best roomy cabin on the ship, with additional suites nearby, which suited everyone's purpose, for Tom, Brett, Clay, Todd, Ben and Red all crammed into their rooms, and they shared her double cot, one man every third night, as this had been pointed out was to become her destiny as their legendary goddess, as she had been mostly known down throughout all the centuries, (or so they said).

The 'invisibles' as she called them were obliging and compatible. They didn't materialize in physical form but she felt them loving her just the same.

Tom was funny and fun to be with, but he did have a cranky side, and didn't like sharing her too much. She knew he definitely loved her for his kisses were long and subjective and left her with no doubt that she could depend on him. She learned he was a divorced man, like Ben, Red, and Clay. Only Brett and Val were bachelors. Tom spoke his mind one early night, after he'd loved her. "Honey, why'd you marry Rob? C'mon, be truthful!"

"Because I love him!"

"What about me?"

"Oh, Tom, you're great! You're second place in my heart!"

"Am I? I'd rather be first."

"How can you be when I'm married to Rob?"

"I'd like to be yours. I'm nuts over you, real crazy for you, baby!"

"And I'm going crazy because I can't 'see' you as Rob can. Why do you need to be invisible all the time!"

"It's our job; covert surveillance. We can do so much more than the ordinary guys can do!"

"Yeah, I realize that! You're phenomenal guys in paranormal guise. But what makes you stay invisible – a magic cloak?"

"Nothing as old-fashioned as that: we use the subnormal power of our minds that's instilled within the reptile brain. Even at birth, we all learned we were different, it's a subversive coding practice based on the twelve auric fields around our bodies. If you'd been trained as we have, even you could do this! In a sense – in your way – you have done it, by astro-visiting and working with us while asleep, and living a double life that way."

"Even though I didn't know I was! And they say we have nine lives, I thought that was an exaggeration!"

"Sure, we have physical, emotional and mental bodies too, as you know. We can 'unzip' one jacket and get into another as easy as changing our clothes."

"Yeah, I get it, you're psychic shape shifters, in a hidden way... Doesn't it make you feel bad? To do things in such a shady, invisible manner?"

"Nope. We're men; we're past all that hype. The junk that sinks in which we do suck up, gets thrown out with the bathwater. We're as thick-skinned as a crowd of rampaging rhinos!"

Janella grinned at the picture this formed in her mind. She said carefully, "And what about the baby boy within? Does he sink too when the going gets tough? Life is hard you know?"

Tom understood what she meant. He had a flexible mind. He spoke gently. "The baby survives, honey. Deep down, we all carry on with our scars and deformities that life brings that sticks in our craw. We're trained to dismiss that."

"I can't dismiss that. I love you – and Rob. It goes deep! You've all turned my world upside down!"

"I know, babe, sure, I told you you were driving me crazy! I feel the same way, can't you forget Rob?"

Janella tried to lighten the mood. "He is my husband you know!"

"So he says – unfortunately!"

She laughed it off, saying teasingly: "You're all superstars to me, you guys! I'm spoiled by all of you!"

Tom left, a little disconsolately, but took it in a gentlemanly way with good grace. "S'long. Let' see each other again soon. Mebbe tomorrow?"

Because she didn't want to let him down she said yes.

Although they weren't too demanding, it was hard to make up her mind who she did like most out of the six men, excluding Rob.

Brett was fulsome and down-to-earth. Clay was exotic, Ben sensual, Red a heart-breaker, Tom protective of her and would do anything for her; he had a good authoritative business sense and memory, and Todd was gentle, dreamy, and artistic. He enjoyed bringing out her creative side by teaching her how to paint portraits.

The trip was only marred by one night when Rob went down with a bad head cold, and he sought another cabin near his wife, which the ship's captain allowed him to have as the Silver Star was not too busy with full bookings on this trip.

Left on her own, apart from the invisibles, tired by the sea air and playing at the ship's small casino, and flirting charmingly with the dashing captain, Emilio Conzsta, Janella turned in early after talking with a cold-doused Rob on her call board.

Ending their conversation she fell straight asleep, whilst her guys played their own card games in the casino room for most of the night. All the men were careful not to give her the cold: she was well looked-after and adored.

The velvet Deittonean night enveloped her. But something awoke her later.

She started up in the room, heart beating, feeling smothered by the deep darkness around her.

Beside her bed, tall as before, stood the being with the alligator face.

"Ah!" She couldn't help the gasp. "You startled me! Why are you here again, what the devil do I call you?"

"Go into trance and listen to me... I have many names little lady. If you remember my last words.... To you I am Voldan of Danak, which is now known as Deitto."

"Whatever your name, why wake me at this hour; it's four in the morning!" Janella moaned.

"Where is your partner, child of the sun-nova?"

"Sleeping on his own with a bad cold next door."

"Then my visit is not ill-timed; I wish to speak with you alone."

"Well, here I am. What have you come to tell me now, alligator man!"

"Do not call me that, child. I am Voldan, remember... I have mentioned to you that many of my people here on Deitto have multiplied with Deitto's females. We are now great in number. This is something you should be worried about... But, first, I promised you that you will know yourself down through the centuries. Sit at the end of your bunk and I will supply pictures in your head."

Puzzled, she did so. Instantly he held, palm upwards, a large grizzled paw of a hand that had what looked like small scales on it, and appearing upon it like magic there were color pictures of her past lives...

She was astonished at the clear array of moving pictures of the times she had been born and died.

At the dawn of time, a Goddess, meant to dwell on Deitto as one forever; in a Neanderthal jungle she had been some kind of queen; in Isis's reign she had been a man – an Egyptian scribe; in Medieval times she had been a witch; in the 15th Century she had been a handmaid; in the French Revolution she had been a Romany gypsy reading fortunes; in the 18th century a harlot; in the 19th century a female Native American Indian Sioux, in the mid-20th century a Bedouin maiden; in the 21st century a wise woman, and in this 22nd century an avatar/guardian and a psychic.

There was one more picture that needed to be shown. She caught a glimpse of some kind of machinery before Voldan snapped his palm shut suddenly and the pictures stopped forming. His short arms, or limbs, dropped to his side.

"Wow! Was that me? What was the machinery one? I only caught half of that last picture!"

"Yes. Your destiny has always been linked with me. The machinery does not concern you yet. Do not ask any more about it. It is taboo to see too much, and you will wonder... I will show you the last picture another time!"

"Can I ask, who are you to me then?"

"Throughout the centuries I have counseled, taught, and advised you. In centuries past I have been your husband, your lover, your friend. We are twinned at the heart, hand and head."

"How come: we are not alike!"

Voldan's mask of a face attempted a smile. "At the very beginning you were once like me – an animal, only prettier, in the heavenly paradise we shared with each other. I created you in different likenesses. The machine you glimpsed, that last picture... you will not like – but I have said enough!"

"You're being so mysterious! But, dear God, don't burn me with awful revelations about my past, why do I need to know all this?"

"You will understand one day after I have – gone!"

"Gone, where? You're not making any sense!"

I will not be harsh on you yet, you are a child still, of the sun-nova, the moon-nova and the stars. One day you will remember your old world, Danak, from this world you call Deitto."

"You said the two were combined, that Deitto had once been called Danak."

"You listen well. There was another one, a smaller planet to the north named Servonis – where you originally came from."

"I'm thunderstruck! I originally come from Servonis? Is this planet still around?"

"It no longer survives in orbit around Danak. It was swallowed by a parallel universe that spawned childless creatures like me. Such creatures as myself finally did raise offspring so sickly that they died off, hence the plan now to produce with Deittonean females, which has worked well, and the females have spawned what they think are true-blue Deittoneans, unaware of the deception. Although some knew, and guessed, when the Lize-nards became known to them. Eons ago I rescued you from it and changed you to the form you are in now. It is no accident that you have been among men most of your life. I watched over you whilst your adopted uncle brought you up."

"He was good to me."

"As I intended he should be. You have been much loved."

"But who were my parents? I was never told about them."

"You were a love child. Your biological father died in a war, your mother in an accident when you were a baby. Your uncle living in Sassinia in Ausina took you on."

"So much to take in! But how could these Lize-nards deceive Deittonean women? Surely they knew what was happening to them! They must have known who they'd conceived with!"

"They did not know. All this was done covertly, by astral intervention, which you are familiar with. The females believed the deed done by their husband's, boyfriends and partners! That is enough for now... I will talk of your mission, to help planet Deitto."

"Yeah, so you've mentioned the Lize-nards plan to multiply with Deittonean females. Who's side are you on?"

"Firmly on your side. We have shared much together and I love you as I have loved you for many millennia."

"Yet you speak as if your people are the bad guys and that we should beware of hybrid children!"

"Yes. Their plans to take over Deitto, offering their ideas to make Deitto a better place for all to be happy in is not true. Under the glitter lies a master plan and these beings must be stopped sooner, rather than later. That is why I appear to you now. To beg you, as a warrior, as a writer, to rally your people to our cause. The beings like me, prefer sex, fire, and everybody's tax money. They care for nothing else."

"And they enjoy people's fear and pain." Janella was remembering the being she had seen standing over Rob's wife in the ambulance. She continued, warming to her theme as a new understanding swept through her. "They gloat over misfortune, offer so much, yet they don't care for us, only for saving Deitto for themselves as their world has gone to dust... I realize now. They create fear and 'accidents' on one side and offer superior goods to everyone like a kind of 'sugared present', encouraging them to spend their tax monies and fall into debt. I see it all now! Thanks Voldan. I was puzzled, but it's clear what is really happening. It's terrible! If children born of decent Deittoneans realize their true hybrid birthright they would panic, not knowing which way to turn. Some may kill themselves in shame! I mean, none of us really love you Lize-nards, do we? All hell will be let loose! Oh God! Oh God! To save us – how can I do this? I'm no avatar! I'm not used to writing bizarre fantasies!"

"You have seen the pictures. You have been one. You are an avatar now, and Deitto's guardian and goddess and natural mother. Writing your stories about this will suffice to alert those to your course. You will be stepping into my labyrinth, and I will follow you and lead you all the way through it! I see I have left you with many thoughts. I will take my leave now. Farewell, sweet child, I shall return."

13

That night was a revelation for Janella. She had this time alone to adjust her thoughts after Voldan's visit. Her invisible lovers took it in turn to come to her, and it would have been Rob's turn tonight, but as he had a head cold, he couldn't share it with her. So she shared it with herself only, her mind calm and clear as her thoughts turned inward to the messages Voldan had given her.

It was enough to make anyone weep. Her planet swept by hordes of hybrid children awakening to their destiny as they grew older, becoming one with the Lize-nards because of their blood bond. She was aware her strength lay in not weeping for her planet, her lovely Deitto that stood so rock-firm in the universe. She knew somewhere, somehow, all was not lost. She just had to draw the people to her and make them see what was really happening under their noses, their hybrid children would need to adjust their shame once they knew their true birthright, so dreadfully linked to the Lize-nards!

Murder and mayhem, law and order, what price for a stabilized world, she wondered?

So she pondered, her writing tablet in front of her. Eventually she wrote a note to remind herself of her thoughts:

'Friends and families, people of our planet, join together in love and harmony. We are being vilified, but we must spread the language of the angels, with no words for hate, and a million words for love! This is what our world is all about: we must be fearless in the face of a warring sky-race enemy that has said they would help us, but instead, have bought us rising prices, less food, water and fuel, and we all know about them. They are called Lize-nards. Some of us have seen them, but we remain, because we are one, and if we all stand together in solidarity of our love for our planet, we will send these beings away to where they originally came from!

'Men, women and children unite around our globe and show this solidarity, beaming 'love', not hate at our invaders offspring. This will help change the status quo.'

'Do not be afraid of accidents happening outside your control: you will be blessed by those in council who know what is really going on, and they will give you advice. Believe me, I know in the end we will win this fight against our enemies who are now around us and who come from the sky, who love this unprecedented heat, and chaos, and destruction! The awful news is that they have mated with Deittonean females, and we must find a way of realizing how to cope with this damning news. This is a story about what is happening now in our surface world, and we must be on the alert, searching steadily for our foe, but doing it with love and acceptance of them being here. Our science will find a way of detecting who has been used against their will and offer solace and understanding, and love, not shame. This will be difficult, but which we can overcome and will overcome this problem, even if we have to destroy the Lize-nard's core leader in order to change the minds of those who follow the beast! But, it will be done with love for everyone on our planet!'

This was her introduction. Then she began her story in earnest and the night without Rob wore on. She called her manuscript "Beastkiller" which started as below:

'A woman speaker was clutching a hover-megaphone in her pink manicured hands. She was dressed immaculately in a bright-red outfit – a warring color – that suited her buoyant gray-blond hair, and she was speaking to hover-cameras, journalists and an expectant crowd of people. Rallying the crowds to her in their moment of crisis on their planet. She cried:

"I can see a river of blood if we go on as we are. I may also see a planet beyond repair, as more hover machines and new inventions in techniques and robots, and new, restricting laws on them come into being, as dictated by our invaders." So echoed the new Capital Leader, thirty-five year old Jjoan Rivers, as she stood in front of robot cameras with her impassioned plea to help keep planet peace and send love around the world, to reconquer their planet from the Lize-nards.

This was her plan, despite male opposition and oppression and she was keen to endorse it.

"Men have ruled – and ruled well, and many men follow my leadership. But an enemy spacecraft approaches us to steal our knowledge – or even our planet. Now it is women's time to show what I can do! I am a woman who works with men towards a greater good for our encumbered, fast-revolving little planet, and I pledge a women's knowledge, a women's philosophy, and a women's war-power to help lead us through this 22nd Century, for freedom from the invaders that have arrived here who will try to assault us! I say, be fearless in the face of all this chaos! Thank you for your applause. Thank you!"

'There was a burst of many hands clapping from those in the crowd watching her. Robotic flashes went off like fireworks flaring in the sky.'

'A male reporter who'd brought along his own camera rose up in front of Jjoan, flashed her, and said loudly: "I'm journalist Martin Ackers. Tell me Miss Rivers how do you plan to handle the men in your official group? Do they follow you implicitly?"'

'It was a sly dig at her superiority and her femininity. She didn't rise to the bait, but forced a charming smile and answered him honestly and smoothly: "I'll 'handle' them as you so sweetly put it with kid gloves, and the odd broom to get them to clear up afterwards! It will be a clean sweep, as they say! We all get along fine and are one big happy family at our group headquarters, and they know I mean business with the invaders – I will do all I can to protect our world!"'

'Martin smiled at her quip. He already like her gamin cheerfulness and her clarity of purpose for her people: she'd past his test. He replied gravely: "Thank you, Miss Rivers, I'm your man! I'll send you the photos I've just taken. Do you want to be photographed with any of your male colleagues?"

"Yes, Ron and Perry, my two right hand men."

"Certainly." He raced to do her bidding, full of admiration.

Later, he had the chance to talk to Jjoan.

"I'm a great fan of yours, Miss Rivers. It sounds rude to ask you so soon, but I have amazing credentials and am at the top of my field, I was wondering if you might take me in as your personal photographer and journalist. I could run some good words in my paper about you and your environmental causes. Not to mention your fighting spirit! I think you're a fabulous and decent lady and I salute you for your stirring speeches. You care so much about your people."

"Why, thank you! I'm overwhelmed by your eagerness. Come to my office in a moment and we'll have a friendly chat!"

"Thank you Miss Rivers."

"Call me Jjoan. Ten moments and I'll be free. You know where to find me?"

"Certainly, Jjoan."

Strangely enough, the pair had hit it off straight away, and they both found, to their surprise, that each liked the other. It led to a further dalliance that night after a candlelit dinner at one of the capital's top restaurants, and the pair became discreet lovers.'

Janella thought some more and outlined her plot further. She had to make it clear planet Asnovae was in great danger! She added more notes...

'Jjoan River's already learns by her superiors that her planet is on a collision course with some kind of magnetic super-star ship that had revealed itself as a deadly enemy to her world. On this star ship are space travelers ready to take over their planet Asnovae which is being pulled into this star ships embracing orbit.

Everyone is frightened of being taken over by these strange beings known as the Lize-ards, whose basilisk stare could freeze the mind in an instant and turn Asnovaenians into mindless zombies. The only people immune to this 'mind' intrusion were children of up to sixteen years of age. There was plans afoot to send them to Asnovae's smaller moon-nova satellite out of harm's way, so they wouldn't be killed or become enslaved by the Lize-nards and used for bad purposes.

Jjoan knew she and her men in her central group had a fight on their hands. She'd ordered every available means of media news to be broadcast to her people – and they had come out in hoards ready to back her up, feeling her genuine protectiveness towards them and their children, who had already been sent away in droves. There were organizations primed, giving out special eyeglasses for the people to wear to shield their sight to save them from the glare of the Lize-ards terrible stares.

Men and woman were willing to hold firm, knowing that 'love' would win the day and send these Lize-ards back to wherever they came from. Such beings as these knew nothing of love. They were conquerors, intent on lust and chaos of her planet – and she wasn't going to allow this. For love she would die or survive, and every man and woman was with her – a united front, a united mind. THEY WOULD WIN!'

On that note Janella yawned and gathered up her story-board and retired to bed and slept soundly, like a baby.

14

After getting over his cold Rob didn't appear too well. On several nights because of severe tiredness, he slept over in the next cabin to theirs, and Tom seemed to take his place more and more.

Tom was a determined, positive lover. He wooed her with ardent, intent, passionate firm kisses, and she found herself wilting under his touch, falling for his charms, his strength, his persistence, and his will.

Although the others remained unseen by her – and Tom was no exception, she felt every inch of him as he lay beside her, sharing the double cot that was really hers and Rob's bed. As the sea rolled by so did she and Tom, and they found themselves falling in love with each other.

What had started as a lighthearted flirtation had turned into something deeper, and they were both mature enough to realize this.

It was a damning predicament for her, as she still loved Rob, but he was so absent at night-times now that it seemed Tom was taking his place.

She found she was pushing the others aside, making way for Tom more and more. Rob noticed and so did Red McBride, who didn't like being 'pushed aside', his ego was injured, and he said: "Try not to ignore me honey, I thought I meant so much to you!"

"You do, Red, but, in truth I love you like a brother! You've been good to me!"

It had been the wrong thing to say; he'd turned his back on her and walked silently away, leaving her wondering if he was still with her or not! She hadn't intended to start a world war, yet everyone seemed to be jealous of each other because she couldn't stop her feelings for Tom from showing!

And Rob complained: "You're not so hot towards me any more! What's up? Have I done something wrong, sweetheart? You seem to be with Tom a lot!"

"Course not! I love you, Rob. It must be the constant attention from the others...who I share my third nights with. Tom probably got his nights mixed up and we've had extra ones by mistake. It's tiring me out as much as your cold has tired you!"

"Yeah, I can't get rid of it; must have been a virus of sorts! Nasty son-of-a-bitch headache still stays with me and makes me feel bad!"

"Maybe it's catarrh as well as the virus that's getting to you!"

She cupped his rugged face in her hands. "I do love you still. Perhaps another night next door might put you right!"

"Sure. I'll try it. Do you mind being with one of the others again? Do your siren's act with them?"

"Okay…, Rob, I must ask, you don't seem to mind that I'm with the others... Doesn't it get to you, sometimes?"

"Sure kid, it does... I get a little jealous of all this man-handling, but I know I can trust you! We all look after you – and I'm the lucky one!" He pinched her waist with a return of his old, charming smile. "One day, we might make a baby!"

"God, not yet! Not with all this alligator business going on! I wouldn't dream of bringing a child into this world whilst they're here!"

"Oh! You're not keen, babe?"

"Not yet anyway! It's too risky!"

"I'd hoped –"

"No, no. Not yet. We'll talk about it another time!"

"I have to point this out… We're legally married sweetheart. I thought you'd like the idea. It would show how much we love each other!"

"You're being very persuasive all of a sudden!"

"When they have a wife as beautiful as you, it's what we men like to make us complete – a child of love! An' it would be my way of keeping you beside me!"

"Rob, I want to enjoy my life with you for a bit, don't get too carried away with this notion!"

"Okay, but we'll talk again about this, I hope..."

"Yes, yes – of course my love!"

On that note she let it go, kissed him soundly and let him out of their cabin to go next door and spend the night. She just hoped he didn't hear her ardent moans when she was with Tom. This was getting complicated and she didn't want Rob to put her under any pressure...

And in the meantime she had a job to do with a story to write. Which she wrote in the day-time, sitting on deck as the waves bounced against the cruise ship churning its way close to the sea using special hover air ducts.

Hover-pad in hand, she typed:

'Continued. "Beastkiller".

'The blast came from the sky and rocked the reinforced building that housed Jjoan River's headquarters. Indoor lights silently flashed red and secret doorways opened in the corridor to allow people to file safely out if necessary, into an escape chute that would take them to a kind of underground bunker where hover-kites would collect them and whisk them off to another secret rendezvous in the city.

The same was being done for citizens all over the little planet.

Green lights flared, showing which city or bay had been hit the most by enemy attack. It seemed to have started all over, with many places falling into dust and debris, and several thousands citizens dead before they could even begin to escape.

At least thousands of the children were safe hiding among their smaller satellite's orbit.

Some would be orphan's before the day was out.

It was grim. Jjoan River's puckered her face into a grimace at the statistics. It was hard to think of sending love waves to her enemies when bloodshed was poured like sticky oil onto the surface of her world, spreading like an indelible stain. What she saw from the satellite pictures looked so real – bodies and buildings littering the ground.

Her first-hand man entered the room. "They're targeting everywhere at once. What can we do?"

"Open a line to the star-ship. I'll talk with their leader. And bring Stacey in."

"Stacey's no good in a situation like this, Jjoan! She's an avatar, not a mediator!"

"Stacey is the best, multi-dimensional spacial psychic robot we have on duty! She'll know how to help us with her great knowledge of warfare. Leave me alone with her; I need to ask certain important questions and do not want to be disturbed!"

"No copying of her answers, no protocol?"

"It will be between her and me. I have a hunch, Ron. Tell others I don't wish to be interrupted for the next sixty moments, please!"

"As you wish. I'll go unlock her holding bay. Don't forget, only you, me and Perry hold the password to her release. She is only to be used in an emergency."

"Don't you think this is one?" Jjoan challenged.

"Yes, you're right. It is" Ron took from his jacket a wallet, flipped it open and keyed in some numbers. There was a whirring sound, and an unseen door whipped silently open.

Stacey, the psychic robot trundled out and stood before Jjoan, whom she recognized by Jjoan's features, eyes and voice. She was a medium height, flesh and artificially boned mind machine, with Asnovae features and fixings including the unusual aspect that all Asnoverians had no eyebrows; she had lips, a nose and her eyes were cobalt gray. She could pass as a true-blue Asnoverian woman any day. Only her voice sounded mechanical.

Ron left discreetly.

Jjoan did not waste any time, but began her strategy. "Stacey. We are at war with the Lize-nard's. How do we defend ourselves from their many attacks?"

"With love, River's, with loving thoughts." The voice-box of this robot sounded hollow, yet it was a women's voice being used.

"It appears not to work; they're attacking everywhere!"

"They, River's? You mean 'he'. 'He' is attacking us."

"How do you mean 'he'? There is more than one of them!"

"It is a trojan horse ruse, River's. There is only one being on board this star ship that is pulling us into its orbit."

"But, I don't understand –? How can this devastation of our planet be caused by one being? Green lights are flashing everywhere showing what has been hit!"

"It is a ruse to make you think this planet is in danger. 'He' has clever devices and techniques to impress damage upon you when it appears deceiving. A special magnetic field is being used to dupe you into believing the carnage and the damage. The satellite photos are fakes. You must speak to this being."

"Right! I intend to! How dare he trick me! Can you put me in touch with his star ship?"

Stacey complied. There was a blip, a whir, and a crusty, rusty voice answered in the language that Jjoan River's spoke on her planet through her interstellar intercom linked to her room.

"I have been waiting for you." It sounded ethereal, as hollow as the robot's. It's creepiness sent a shiver down Jjoan's back.

She swallowed and cleared her throat, demanding haughtily: "Whatever you are, why do you attack us?"

"I am a Lize-nard named Assiard and master of this ship. My aim is to conquer your world with my superior weapons. You will not resist me!"

"Oh, we will, I will drive you away in hordes if I have to! We do not surrender to raiders raised on your planet Celatine." She thought she'd try a different track. "You're planet is dying. Do not be foolish. We can help you and you can teach us new ways to live, and ease the strain on our burgeoning planet. Why not join us instead of fighting us?"

There was a harsh bark of a laugh. "You speak as a woman to offer loaded bargains! A man would not haggle so soon, but cheat and lie his way forward! How can I trust you?"

"Our planet is in chaos itself. But we can give shelter and 'love'. I offer this to you; one turn for another."

"Then you are a foolish woman! My resources are many, and I shall win!"

"I am told you are only a single being; can we not compromise –"

"Whether I am single or not, I will pulp this planet, unless..."

"Unless, what?"

"Shelter and love is not on my agenda, however, if you offer yourself to me – that would suit my purpose!"

"You want me as some kind of consort, or concubine?" Jjoan sounded appalled and aghast at the idea. "Never! How dare you! What kind of beast are you?"

"A non-human, almost an animal. I know a lot about you: you are a single spinster, now a Capital Leader who works with admiring men, and your people love you. I could claim you now. I have that power to transport you to my star ship against your will!"

"I am not in your bargain!"

There followed a ferocious growl of rage and her signal to the star ship was abruptly cut off.

Shaking badly with this astonishing interchange, she had to resign herself to a mental defeat, and to send robot Stacey back into her holding bay.

She had a feeling she would hear more from this being before the day was out. And she knew now it was up to her; she would have to give an answer to save her planet and her people. This being was expecting it.

She grimaced. Thank God it had been a private conversation with robot Stacey hearing it and recording it, as she had ordered, discreetly.

There seemed only one way out.

She sat abruptly, her eyes still registering her horror at this unexpected turn of events.

What the devil had she been talking to?

15

Janella sensed Tom was getting besotted with her. He wrangled it to be by her side nearly all the time and she felt even Rob must realize what was going on. Her guilt over this made her edgy with Rob.

At the ship's dinner table one lunch time when they were dining together, Rob spoke apropos of nothing: "I think Tom's getting too forceful with you, and you don't seem to mind his attentions!"

She'd been sipping hot soup d' bouillon and paused, flushing a little under Rob's intensive scrutiny.

"Whatever do you mean? Tom's not taking advantage of me!"

"I suss he god-damned well is."

"Don't be silly –"

He leaned over deliberately and placed a hand on her arm that held the sloppy soup to her lips. She shook it off in vexation and the soup splashed onto the white tablecloth.

"Now look what you've made me do!"

Rob didn't apologize. He looked grave, his face set in determined hard lines.

"You like him a lot, don't you?"

"He's okay." She shrugged, not looking him in the eye as he was with her.

Rob sighed. "You get tetchy when I speak about him. D'yuh feel guilty about something? C'mon Janella, spit it out. I know how you feel about that ass-hole! Yuh can't fool me no matter how god-damn hard you try to hide it!"

"Oh, I'm off if you're going to talk like that!" She stood up so abruptly her floating chair lopped sideways and a waiter hurried over to right it for her.

She scurried away as if she'd been struck in the face, leaving Rob to order another bottle of Chablis – for himself.

After this, she spoke to Brett Kerr, for he was the oldest in her group and she trusted his wisdom.

She had been standing at the prow of the cruise ship, her favorite place, and Brett had joined her. In his unseen way he placed his arms around her and gave her a loving, brotherly hug.

He spoke in his warm, twangy, earthy Ausina voice: "G'day love! Why the long face? You all right Skipper! You look like you're under a snapper attack an' the blighter's bitten yuh!"

Janella gave him a wan smile that didn't meet her golden eyes. They looked pinched, and sad. "Uh, what's a snapper?"

"A snapper? An alligator, little skipper!"

"Oh!"

"What gives, honey? You seem miles away?"

She glanced at the shimmering misty sea without seeing it. "It's Tom."

"Ah, thought so. You're getting it together, aren't you? Skimming too close to the waves, huh?"

His knowledge of this didn't surprise her. She asked point blank: "What do I do, Brett? I love you all, yet I love both Tom and Rob in a way that really hurts me. I'm torn in two by both of them!"

Her distress was evident.

Brett considered. In his twangy voice he advised: "Let's put it this way honey. Who d'you love the most at this moment in time?"

She leaned against him with a sob in her throat. "It's Tom! God help me Brett – it's Tom! I can't get him out of my head! And I think I've upset Red!"

"Nah, Red's okay."

"Honest, he's not! He walked away from me because I likened him to a brother and not a lover! This whole mix n match business is driving me crazy!"

"Red'll come round. He loves you too much, kid. Don't worry about him! Let's sort your 'dilemma' out; you'll jus' have to come clean with Rob!"

"He looked daggers at me at the lunch table just now! Put me off eating my soup!"

"Want me to have a word with him – man to man?"

"What would you say?"

"Hah, remind him what a superwomen you are! He lets us share you as we've done before, he can do it again. It's a male thing, to get jealous when you're hitched to a beautiful woman. Thank Christ females don't get testosterone trouble, it's all trade and trousers for us!"

He was so funny, she had to grin in a watery way. "I hope I'm not too much 'traded', as you claim! Thanks for the advise Brett."

As she said this a trance came upon her. She found and patted Brett's shoulder lightly saying: "I'll speak with Rob and Tom later and I'll see you tonight, Brett!"

"Sure baby. Try not to get too upset. I'm around out here if you need me."

Janella nodded, her throat tight. Trance took over and she foresaw Rob swilling down a bottle of alcohol... The vision didn't bode well, and it troubled her. He rarely drank wine, only bourbon, sometimes beer.

She opened her eyes and came out of her trance now knowing the outcome. Yet her sense of unease continued –

She had also foreseen something wrong with this ship's engines.

16

To clear her mind, Janella got out her writing tablet from her bag and continued with 'Beastkiller'.

'Jjoan Rivers often took a fifteen minute nap in the afternoon. It set her up for the rest of her busy, energetic day. This morning, after her curt talk with the Lize-nard she took her nap early.

When she awoke her mind was clear. She was wide awake and thinking fast.

She knew what to do, and she was dead calm inside about her actions.

There was a pill in her pocket of her coat, to take in times of death or danger. All the top people had one of these, kept safe upon their clothing. She wasn't planning to take hers yet. Things would have to get pretty hairy for that to happen!

Yet she knew she would have to take it to save her people and her planet, if need be.

Resolutely she walked to her desk and made a note on her embossed paper pad, then tapped her intercom button that put her through straight to Ron's office. He wasn't in, and she passed on a command knowing he would receive it with mixed feelings.

"Ron, very important, do not disturb me for the next 120 moments please. This is an order. Thank you." It gave her a few hours.

Then she opened the secret door to robot Stacey's holding bay, and as the robot glided into Jjoan's office, the Capital Leader said abruptly: "Stacey. You're with me. I need you as back-up. Are all your monitor's working?"

"Charged and ready, ma'am." Replied the almost-human female robot in her sepulchral flat woman's voice.

"Good. Stand by. We're going on a spaceship adventure. And I may certainly need your help, Stacey."

"Yes, ma'am, I'm standing by."

"Good. Wish me luck and diplomacy, Stacey."

"Yes, ma'am."

Jjoan looked around her familiar tidy office, wondering if she'd signed all her papers for today. She hesitated, glancing almost shyly at the robot.

Sensing her emotions, Stacey asked: "Are you scared ma'am?"

"Yes, Stacey. For myself, this time. Shall we go?"

17

Janella frowned, stopping her writing, thinking of something else. What could be wrong with this cruise ships engines that she'd sensed a moment ago? They were skimming above the waves okay when she looked overboard just now.

She wondered if she should tell someone. The captain was on the bridge at that time of night. She decided she'd mention this to him, but didn't really want to give her medium-ship away knowing that some people didn't believe in trance or psychic happenings.

A large hand covered her hand and she realised Red was standing beside her with his imposing, princely presence. As a joke, because he'd told her he had straw-colored hair, she'd nicknamed him 'sun-king'.

"Honey?"

"Hi sun-king."

"Sorry I walked away. You hurt my pride. I slipped sideways for awhile."

"I'm sorry, Red. I think the worlds of you. I didn't know what I was saying!"

"S'okay honey. I'm over it! You love Tom more than me, don't you?"

"Intuitive, aren't you?"

"Can't help realizing it honey."

She bent her head. Red noticed her downcast face. Unseen, she felt her chin lifted up. A gentle, but long giant kiss followed. Red was a devil of a charmer, and she had to grin when he'd finished. She had a sense he was grinning too, a lazy smile lighting up what she assumed to be a very handsome face. He had such a dramatic personality and, at that moment, she was very drawn to him, to his love of life, his magnanimous spirit, and his child-like belief in wooing her back.

"Oh, Red, you make me feel good again!"

"Pleased to help ma'am, but try not to muck me about – I melt around you!"

She lightly punched him where she thought his torso was, and he puffed out a breath. "Ouch, miss bossy boots! Are we friends again?"

"Always, Red, always. I'll see you at dinner, yeah?"

"S'long kid!" She had the sense he was giving her a laconic wave. He liked to play the captain. Which reminded her of where she was headed, the bridge.

A little doubtful she walked to the bridge and climbed the steps. Emillio Conzsta was standing beside the huge switchboard that housed all the cruise ships implements.

He turned in surprise at her approach. "Madam, this is a pleasure..."

"I'm sorry to bother you, but I was being shown the massive engine room by one of your men, and I'm no engineer, but I seemed to sense something not working well with engine number two. I hope I'm not wrong, but it seems to have shut down."

"Strange. Why didn't my man report this to me?" The captain glanced at his controls.

"He er, took sick, so I came here instead."

"Sick – what is his name?"

"I – didn't ask!"

"It's very strange – I have only just noticed it – you're right! Engine number two has shut down. The lights have started to blink telling me so. I can see the trans-valve is interfering with the air contra-flow propeller. Maybe it needs a new decoder? Will you excuse me whilst I get my men onto it Madam, and step outside now? And thank you for telling me!"

"That's okay, I'm leaving anyway. I know I shouldn't really be here! Will we be all right?"

"Perfectly all right, madam. This is a strong air-cruising floating ship that was thoroughly overhauled whilst in her dock – she won't sink!"

"Thanks for that good news! Goodnight captain."

"Goodnight madam. I must call my engineers. Thank you for telling me!"

Janella left him and walked down to the lower cabins. On the way she again met Red, this time with Ben. They were smoking small cigarillo's which contained narcotics. It was all the rage to smoke these. She knew it was them by the glow and sweetish smell of their cigarillo's, and their faint signals they sent out to her. She'd taken them by surprise, she could tell this as well. "Hi guys."

From leaning over the ship's rail, Red straightened up. He said, nonchalantly: "Hi doll. You've spoken to me already today, but Ben's feeling left out of it all now!"

"Oh, Red, stop teasing! Ben, sorry! You know why I'm so mute today, I expect Red's told you! I can't help how I feel about Tom! Not now everyone knows!"

There was such pathos in her voice that Red sighed and gave her a loving hug. "Sorry, sweetheart! I know how you feel. We're jus' grumpy old men, eh Ben?"

Ben grimaced. He was as much a lady charmer as Red in a down-to-earth kind of way. He said logically: "You and Tom will both have to come clean with Rob, darling!"

It was Janella's turn to make a face. "Rob spoke to me at dinner, but I ran away, looking for solace from Tom. Do you know where he is?"

"Working out in the gym with Clay. Come on, we'll go help you find him!" Ben understood her. He took her hand and squeezed it warmly. Rob took her other hand and did the same.

She marched off with them, a pretty young woman, seemingly alone enjoying her walk along the deck, yet you'd be puzzled to see two glowing cigarillo's held in invisible hands as the trio walked along by with her.

In the gym they found Tom had left, but Clay was still working out going by the groaning and creaking of the muscle machine!

"Hi guys, hi baby!" Clay's sweaty hand ruffled her hair, giving her a clue as to which exercise machine he was on. It was the arm pull down, strengthened on tension number seven. Clay was working hard on his biceps. As she was standing beside it Clay reached out and gave her a hug and a kiss. "How's you, sweetheart?"

She could feel the sweat on his warm hands. "Out of sorts. I'm looking for Tom, Clay. Do you know where I can find him?"

"In his cabin, I expect. S'pect yuh need to see him about you know what?"

Janella sighed, word got around! "If you mean 'me and Tom', then I do! You know too, then?"

"Sure baby. I'll be backing you if Rob turns nasty about it! You can count on me!"

"He's never been nasty to me yet."

"We men can turn funny y'know? Especially where women are concerned! Our brains go to our pants!"

"I'll remember that. Brett said something like it. Advice please, what would you say to Rob?"

"Say that none of us can help how we feel for each other, and to ask him to come round and accept what has happened, you can't help it."

"That sounds practical anyway!"

"That's me, baby, tenacious, self-indulgent, pleasure-loving and practical! Take my advise and stay firm! On the tenacious bit – gimme a kiss to show you still love me!"

Clay was the tallest. She sensed him stand up and raised on tiptoe to give him one, then Red, and then Ben who whispered in her ear: "Count on my help too, darling!"

"Okay, thanks guys. I'm off to find Tom!"

18

Tom was in his cabin, talking to Todd. Todd was the wise guy of the group. He wore a self-confident facade under a lonely cloak and Janella, sensing this, had always gone out of her way to befriend him and make him feel better about himself.

She waltzed up to Todd and gave him a loving, gentle kiss, stroking his long hair, which was shoulder length.

"Hi lovely, you take my breath away!" She sensed Todd's smile and thought he was in high spirits for once.

"Todd, do you mind if I have a word with Tom, in private please?"

"Sure, I was jus' gonna go." Todd's artistic voice floated over to the cabin door, and she realised he'd walked away. He was very goal-orientated and enjoyed good living and good food! He was also very spiritual and a true traditionalist!

"Thanks Todd. See you at dinner?"

"Yeah, I'm getting hungry, Janella, s'long! By the way – if you wear one of your evening gowns tonight, I'll put on my tuxedo-in-one-suit!"

"You don't wear a tuxedo in this day and age, surely? That's so old-fashioned!"

"Remember, Janella, I'm an old-fashioned traditionalist! An' when I walk alongside you I like to look the gentleman's part!"

"Will do, Todd! I understand!"

The cabin door creaked to as Todd left them.

She faced where she knew Tom to be standing, by his bed. "We need to speak about us, Tom!"

"Hell, honey, I know. Come here! I want to hold you and never let you go!"

She cleared her throat. "Come to me. I'm not going to bed with you yet!"

"Aw honey, you drive a man nuts! I want you!"

"So do I, but this is serious now, isn't it, Tom? We need a strategy to work something out about us, for Rob's sake, and ours."

Janella found her arms pinned in a sudden hug. He'd crossed the room to her.

"Janella, I love you!"

"And I love you, too." She mouthed, after he'd kissed her passionately. She felt her blood levels rise with her need to be beside him. "We can't go on like this. Rob will have to be told!"

"Yeah, you must tell him soon. I'll be with you on this. It's my problem too."

"When shall we tell him?"

"Soon!" He smooched her lips and lit up his longing within her. She found herself responding and she'd meant to stay calm!

They ended up on the bed anyway...

Dinner on board the cruise ship was around seven in the evening. Janella found she had around sixty moments to get on with her story 'Beastkiller', so she got out her pad and began to write. After Tom's ultimatum it refreshed her to think of something else other than her and Tom's present dilemma.

'Jjoan and robot Stacey found themselves standing in the inside of a spacious star ship. It was wide and glowing with instruments, hidden panels and dials, yet there was only one visible floating seat to take it's owners commands from.

And in that seat sat Assiard the Lize-nard. He smirked his long jaws into a parody of a smile as Jjoan Rivers and Stacey massed into being under a surreal mist that announced their developing entrance.

Standing on the landing pad with special glasses on so the Lize-nrd's gaze didn't turn her into a zombie, Jjoan looked around her in some wonder. Despite everything, her people were not yet space explorers. They were only beginning to learn of its vast matter and its graphic spacial ocean that swirled around their world, and they had only managed to travel to their moon-orbiting satellite where the children of Deitto had been taken to for safety.

When she saw Assiard smirking at her she nearly fainted in alarm.

He looked frightening. A body of ten foot in height with a long extending alligator chin was glaring at her with hot, red, baleful eyes, watching her startled, defensive reaction with animal-like glee.

In her language the frightful creature said: "Here comes the capital leader herself! What shall we do with her, hmmm?"

"Nothing bad I hope!" Jjoan plucked up courage and found her voice and used it, as she would have used it at public meetings and crowded halls. "You are Assiard I believe, a being very much on your own from what I can see here. Why are you attacking our planet? I haven't the statistics yet, but it looks bad for us!"

"Yes, I am Assiard; you're planet is safe at the moment; I was merely showing you what I could do if you do not agree to my terms, woman counselor."

She raised her chin. "And what are those? Your star ship is scooping down and drawing my planet into its orbit. Why?"

"Because I have the power to do this – and worse. You would be wise to heed my arguments. I could take over your planet as easily as this -" Assiard clicked his fingers, or what looked like fingers. He appeared to have only four.

"What do you want?"

"You!"

"Me? Whatever for?"

"To co-habit and breed with! You have a good pedigree. We could bring forth hybrid children to help my race survive again. A continuity you could say! You will comply with this!"

"NEVER! You are mad to think I will!"

"Ah, you will, because I know where the children are – upon your moon satellite thinking they are safe. I will not make a safe world for them! You are warned to take me seriously. Very seriously."

"You're inhuman! Inhuman! If you think the children – you cannot use them against us like this! You're bluffing!"

"I am deadly serious. If I attack now, the children will still die with you, once I have chosen the best ones and turned them against you, the females to be used as hybrid mothers, their children sired by me! As I am, as you see, the only surviving member of my race – apart from those on your planet's surface. I can do this, and I will. Be my consort and I'll help you save your planet from extinction and give your world everything it needs, to please everyone."

"I do not believe what you are saying or claiming. You can't take us over just like that to save your own soul!"

"I admit my intentions are not honorable. You have come to me. I take your willingness to talk with me as your answer! Come here."

You cannot do this to us, to me! I will not be taken by force!" Jjoan stood open-mouthed, hardly able to believe her ears.

The sepulchral tones of robot Stacey's voice spoke up: "Grand leader, I sense he speaks the truth. Our planet does need saving and so do the children. This being means what he says!"

In her mind Jjoan thought wildly: "What do I do, robot?"

In robot Stacey's mind her thoughts too came back to Jjoan. The Deittoneans called this mind language 'shadow whispers' and everyone on Deitto could do it apart from the children. They would be taught the method later when they came of age.

"Kill him. Use me. I'm primed as you have ordered me. Do not take you're poison tablet yet because you may not need it; I will save you!"

Jjoan Rivers eyes flashed with determined fire. One thing she was sure of here; this being didn't know her world used mind thoughts to each other sometimes. Assiard was looking from the robot to Jjoan, wondering at their hesitation, still smirking expectantly.

"Then do it! I'm prepared to die with you Stacey!"

"My leader, I will survive the explosion. My records will show the planet what you have done for us!"

Jjoan closed her eyes, blotting out her foe. Tightly, with a sob in her throat, she mind-ordered bravely:"Do it Stacey – NOW – I am prepared! Good luck! "

A beam of light shot out of the robot's forehead blinding the waiting being that was Assiard. He threw gnarled hands up to shield his eyes and staggered back onto his mechanical instruments, knocking some of the levers back: "Aaarrhh!"

There was a whirr of sound as the star ship leapt forward, with lights glowing on the instrument panel and a heavy-looking loading bay door was beginning to open as Assiard fell onto his ship's controls...

Robot Stacey continued with her light beam, directing it's fierce flame at Assiard's long face.

His controls were melting, instruments whirring and catching alight behind him, and suddenly, from rim to rim the whole craft was aflame with fire!

Jjoan felt the heat exploding around her. Her hair began to frizz as she was blasted off her feet.

Stacey the robot caught her in her arms, with both of them on fire, flying through the air and making it through the loading bay hatch, she carried Jjoan's body home...

Assiard's ship exploded in white-hot flames, and after one single scream of pain Jjoan had fainted in her robot's arms...'

19

Because they'd been together earlier, Tom cried off being with Janella that night, and Rob took Tom's place, but it was the middle of the night when they heard the explosion. The cruise ship's siren began to ring, urgently awakening everyone who was in bed and sleeping soundly, apart from Rob and Janella who were lying awake after their first row.

Before this happened Janella had been having a serious tête-à-tête with Rob.

After a quick union she'd sat up in the bed and asked abruptly: "Rob, do you do this hide n seek business?"

Blatantly, tongue in cheek, he replied, realizing what she meant: "Hide n seek – what's this? I'm under cover now, with you!"

"I didn't mean in bed, I meant, can you do what your friends do – vanish into nothing form and become invisible!"

"Nope. Not my line, I've told you that before. What's yours, sweetheart?"

"You know it; I'm a love doll."

"Cheer up, it can only get worse if yuh let it! Which you have!"

"How do you mean! I'm keeping to my side of the bargain!"

"I don't think so! You're side of the bargain as you quaintly put it, involves Tom, doesn't it?"

"It involves everyone. Don't be so bitter!"

"Hah, I have a reason to be; you must love Tom more if you don't wanna start a baby with me!"

"I'd certainly settle for one man to love first –"

And that was when the explosion happened...

"What the hell's going on?" Rob was staring at his hover-clock. The light in their room had changed from a mellow gold to a luminous pale blue as if they were caught in a misty moon lit night.

"Damned if I know!" Yet Janella remembered the broken number two engine, and she wondered.

Instinct moved her to add: "Let's get out and get dressed Rob. I sense trouble."

Their cabin door opened and Rob said: "It's okay, its the boys."

Janella sometimes forgot he could see Tom, Brett, Clay, Todd, Red and Ben. She still couldn't!

Tom had just closed their cabin door when it opened again. A uniformed man in seashore white shorts stood in the doorway.

"Very sorry to disturb. The captain wants everybody up and out."

"Why, man?" Rob asked as he slid into his trousers.

"Engine trouble, sir, and we may have hit a mine. It blew up underwater as we passed over it, we think. Maybe some kind of sabotage. Sorry! We need to have a roll call and gather everyone on deck. Thank you!"

"Are we sinking?" Rob asked urgently.

"No sir, we were skimming high and she's a strong ship, but damage has been done to pipes lying under the sea!"

"If it's sabotage man, no nuclear sub could have hidden in these shallow waters. It must have been some kind of acoustic signature, probably positioned and set on this ship's engine, which blew as we passed by!"

"Agreed sir, it's worrying; are we ready to leave?" The sailor was about to turn away.

Something or someone sent him sprawling back into Janella and Rob's room with a startled oath. He crashed into the wall and slithered to the floor, his neck broken like a rag doll.

Janella put a hand to her mouth. Rob swore and swung down beside the sailor to check him out.

There was a red weal across his face as if he'd been slapped by something scaly.

When Rob stood back up the slug gun was in his hand that he had used when they were on their honeymoon. "Move back, Janella. There's something out there!"

20

In the commotion in her cabin, Janella's writing block had fallen on the floor on the 'Continuing "Beastkiller" page'. She had written the final chapter the evening before when she'd had a night to herself. Although, with this attack she'd had no time to read and correct it yet, it began:-

'The body on the hospital bed had bandages tied all around the face, chest and arms.

Martin Ackers sat by the bed, his hand gently holding Jjoan Rivers bandaged hand lightly, so as not to hurt her.

She could see through the eyelets they had left, although her sight was a little scarred and dim.

"Jjoan, my love..." Martin was almost crying. "Why the hell did you do it? Couldn't someone else have burnt and bust up that damn ship? It was a terrible brave thing to do! Why you?"

Despite the stiffness of her bandages she found a croaky voice and said faintly: "Because it was up to me. No one else would have volunteered. I did it because I cared so much that everyone should be safe! It knew about the children, threatened me with them if I didn't obey it..." Her voice, tired now, dropped to a whisper. The drugs were working in her system, easing such a terrible searing pain.

"Couldn't you have left that damn robot to do it for you?"

"Oh, stop saying 'damn'! Flatly, no. Stacey helped me escape. Is she badly scorched?"

"Fuck! She's a bloody robot, woman! Of course she'll be all right! It's you I'm worried about!"

"Dear Martin, don't worry about me. I'll live! Stacey took the full brunt of impact. She shielded me from the worst – and got me out of that star ship, away from that awful, hideous red-eyed being! I'm lucky we had her and I took her with me. Otherwise I'd be dead!"

"Don't say that, woman! I want to ask you to marry me! I'd do it here and now if you weren't in so much pain!"

"Did you say what I thought you'd said?"

"Damn right! Jjoan Rivers, you brave, stubborn woman, will you marry me?"

"There's no need to shout, man, and you keep saying 'damn' – I can hear you – I've still got ears!"

"Christ, Jjoan – you mean that, really,?"

"Of course, when I get out of here – not before – I want to be a proper bride for once, even if my hair is going streaky-gray and burnt to a frazzle!"

"Oh, Jjoan!" Martin bent over and kissed her bandaged forehead. "You are such a wonderful woman! I love you! You've won the battle and saved our children and our planet from harm! WELL DONE! I'm going to really write about this piece of good news, and your pictures going t'be at the top of the page! Even if I have to manually stick it there myself, and override what I've originally written!'"

21

In the disarrayed cabin, Janella sensed Tom take her hand and move her away from the body of the sailor lying at an awkward angle on the floor.

Rob disappeared into the night with his slug gun. She heard the sounds of a struggle and cried out:

"Rob, what's happening? Are you all right?

Tom spoke in her ear: "I think he's in trouble... Hang on, I'm going to materialize. So are the others. Don't be too alarmed!"

Suddenly, the tiny cabin was full of six men crowding around the large king-size bed.

Tom Wilson was nearly the tallest with mellow white hair and brown eyes. Clay Coleby was really tall with blue eyes, Brett Kerr was shorter with green eyes, Todd Rogers was as tall as Tom and burly in a healthy way, with long light brown hair tied back at the nape of his neck, Ben Swift was roughly Tom's height, also with brown eyes, and handsome-faced Red McBride was just a centimeter shorter than Todd. They were all tanned and wore vests and shorts.

"Good God!" Janella was understandably amazed at the transformation. Six handsome men! And they all loved her!

Before anyone could stem her amazement, something came through the door.

And it wasn't Janella's helpful Lize-nard friend, Voldan.

It was a group of about three mean-looking Lize-nards, and they began to attack her guys, who had to put up their hands to their faces to avoid the beasts club-like weapons.

Before Janella could scream for help, a scaly, long-fingered hand blocked her mouth and nose so she couldn't breath properly, and she had to close her eyes, hearing the sounds of a harsh-to-the-death fight going on between her boys and these half-beings, for she knew what they were, Lize-nard thugs, and they were under attack!

A scalloped hand closed around her wind-pipe with a crushing grip. She gasped, gurgled in pain, trying to lash out with her free hand, almost feebly for her. She hit out at nothing, the being was whisking her off her feet as if she was an empty sack. It's strength was incredible and she feared for her men, whose curses she could hear broadly, as they too were slammed down.

She was roughly bundled outside, resisting all the time, her inner strength finally coming to her aid, and flung against the port-side deck rails, nearly cracking her right rib. The being was trying to shove her overboard and she groaned with the pain of her stinging rib just as the ship began moving again! It seemed number two engine had now been made good.

She fought tremendously then, with a rage inside her at this atrocity that went deeper than words. With hands, fingernails, feet, and knees she tried hard to gouge and hit back, her avatar's rage coming to the fore.

But she was forced to clutch the rails as she was finally chucked over...

She clung on grimly to the port-side rail, teeth clenched, but the being deliberately and crushingly prized her fingers away from her handhold and she had to let go and dropped into the glassy sea.

At least she could swim. She choked sea-water and splashed as much as she could to stay afloat, terrified that Rob and the others would be killed.

There followed splash after splash after splash. Blinded by the water and the spray she swam towards where she'd heard the first splash.

"TOM! ROB! BEN! Oh – where are you? HELP! HELP!" She coughed, gulping sea water that had a nasty, salty, brackish taste, the dirty waste bilge of a tainted sun-scored sea.

No one on board the moving ship seemed to have heard her cries.

She'd never felt so alone and frightened in all her life.

A wet hand touched her arm. "It's Tom, Janella! Stay still a minute, sweetheart! I'm going to see if I can find the others. Hold on to this!" He handed her a hover life-belt which would lift her out of the water slightly and stop her sinking, and also, a special water torch, which she flicked on, highlighting the dark, oozy water around her.

She gasped: "Tom... Find Rob!"

"Okay – look – there's two of 'em!" The torches beam had picked out Clay and Rob, and in the surreal light of a full moon-nova Tom swam strongly to where they both were threshing in the water, a little the worse for fighting.

Janella looked for Brett, Todd, Red and Ben. She heard splashes behind her and knew, with relief, that the other men in her group were all right, for now, above the roar of surging water she could hear them calling her name.

She noticed something to her right. Was it her imagination or did she spy land ahead? Some kind of jutting cliff-top was looming out of the night. She shouted out as loud as she could despite swallowing more brackish salt water: "Tom? I'm heading for that land on the northern horizon. Can you make it there with the others?"

"Sure can!" She hardly heard Tom's faint reply above the choppy sea waves. He shoved his hand above the water to show he was still afloat.

Janella pulled a string on the hover life-belt and it propelled her gently towards the dark shoreline.

Somehow they all managed to propel themselves above the waves and gain a foothold on dry land.

Tom had found Rob who had almost drowned as, by the looks of his rugged features, he'd put up quite a fight with their night-time invaders.

Janella fumbled at her life-belt, deflating it, and dragged herself, wet and shivering in her dressing gown wrap over to Rob.

"You okay, Rob?"

He nursed his head in his hands, blood dribbling blackly from cuts on his face. Even in the dark she knew he had taken a pummeling. She threw her arms around him and he cringed in pain from her touch.

"Ouch – careful!"

"What did it do to you? They tried to murder us! I believe it was a plan; they shut down the ships number two engine, tried to blow up the ship and got that sailor to alert us, then they attacked!

"You're right. It was a set-up. That beast-thing knocked the gun from my hand and blacked my eyes. Damn near killed me. Tom happened by and we knocked it out between us."

"I wasn't expecting this." Janella spoke apprehensively.

"Me neither."

"What do we do now? The captain and his crew won't miss us 'till morning. Unless they've done a roll-call and overlooked our not being there!"

"We wait here, build a fire and get warm. The beings think they've killed us but I've sent an SOS to the capital and Hopgood-Royce. Some one will come, pick us up. Don't worry, the ships traffic in this area can get pretty dense, we'll be okay. Rescue will come soon."

"How'd you manage to do that? Send for help so quickly?"

"Snatched your hover writing pad and sent an emergency message signal on it before I rushed out to do battle."

"I didn't see you do it."

"You were too dumbstruck to notice, but I managed it, and help will come! Trust me?"

"Of course, Rob, I love you!"

His gravelly expression changed and became hard: "Huh, that true? I didn't think you did, honey!"

There was bitterness in his voice which sounded as haggard as he looked.

"I love you all –"

"Don't give me that bullshit, you love Tom more than me!"

Sensing his mood she rose up, but he grabbed her hand strongly. "You're Mrs McKen – remember ME darling? I am your husband!"

"Don't be sarcastic. The others will hear!"

"Shall I have it out with Tom then, 'bout you and me an' him?"

"You're not being very nice to me. This fight has turned you bad!"

"You aren't being good to me either – swarming off with Tom most nights!"

"This isn't the time to talk about how we feel for each other! You do pick your moments, I'm not your scapegoat!"

"How I feel, huh? This time's as good as any. I want to start a baby with you, and god-dammit I will, whether you like it or not!"

"Don't be selfish, Rob – I didn't have you down for that! You can't demand that of me yet! We've only been married a short while!"

"So? You've been swanning around with everyone but me! Don't MY wishes count!"

"You're getting jealous!"

"It's more than jealousy – it's important to me we start a family – for my sake! It's something that has to be done!"

"And what if I don't want to? Why is this so all-important to you?"

"Because you said you loved me!"

"But, why this persistence? Did your ex-wife allow this too? Is that why you have so many kids? Aren't you being a bit 'baby-talk' heavy? Read my lips – I don't want to yet?"

Rob pursed his lips, his green eyes flashed darkly. "Don't get me angry, doll!"

"Hey, Rob, leave her alone! Talk to me about it if you have to!"

Tom was suddenly beside Janella. He took hold of her other arm. "Ignore that horny jerk, Janella, come with me! I'll see you okay!"

Hurt and ashamed, she would have done, but Rob stood up too and raised his gun at Tom.

"Mother-fucker – go to hell! She married me, and she'll give me what I ask for – and screw the lot of yuh!"

"No Rob, I won't," Janella found her voice. "I'm off with Tom if you're going to talk like that! Simmer down! You've really shown your true colors now! That fight has brought out your jealousy over me and Tom."

"You've changed towards me as soon as I mention 'babies'? "

"Yeah, because I love Tom more than you! He's not 'pushing' me like you are!" She blurted truthfully. "Whatever has gotten into you, Rob?"

"Tom has! I hate the bastard! He's split us up! I'll get you Tom, good n' hard!" And Rob sprang at Tom, who let go of Janella's arm, stood his ground, and swung a fist at Rob, knocking him back onto the shingled ground. Rob's gun fell on the shingle.

They rolled over together, pummeling hard.

"What you doing, ass-hole, taking my wife away from me, you bastard?"

Tom panted: "Don't be a fool, Rob! For Janella's sake we can sort this out without slugging our brains out, man!"

They broke off, got up and circled each other warily.

"We were friends once, Rob. I don't need to fight you to show how much she loves me better!"

"I'll fight for what's mine!" They grappled again and both slipped over, still rolling and pummeling each other.

Clay, Red, Brett and Ben all ran up to try and separate them. Todd went and stood beside a shivering Janella and held her in his arms, thoughtfully shielding her from the fight.

Somehow the others managed to dis-tangle the two men and separate them, both fighting mad, their blood up.

"We could see how things were going." Brett lumbered up to Janella. "Something had to break, and Rob did first! For the last two simmering weeks you could have cut the god-damn tension between these two with a knife! We didn't know how to tell you!"

"It's all my fault!"

Tom, cut across the left eye, held her in his arms. "It's out in the open now; I love you Janella, and I know you love me. Despite being married to him there's not a thing he can do to separate us. It's your choice, honey – him, or me?"

Janella nodded. "It's you, Tom."

She walked over to where Rob was dusting down his wet clothes. Sand was sticking to him, as it was on Tom.

"I did love you. Yet I realise you love your wife more. I can tell, it's in you're voice when you speak about her sometimes... Why so urgent to make a baby with me?"

"Because I needed to tell you the truth!"

"What truth, Rob? What do you mean?"

He took a deep, painful breath. "I'm a hybrid myself Janella. Just like you talked about in the CL's office. We're the kind of people you'd detest if I'd told you the truth. We're part Lize-nard. Now do you understand. Our capital leader knew this, but we didn't tell you. My wife is a hybrid too, and our children; we're part of a new race developing in this world!"

"Oh my God! Rob – this is so –"

"Awful, I know."

"Have I got this right? You – you're trying to raise as many hybrid babies as you can for these terrible creatures who are rapidly taking over our planet? You're nothing like them! You haven't an alligator's face!'"

"Yeah, it's true. They don't do it themselves when in an astral state – they can't. They have to insert their dye, you know? The insert phial is filled with our DNA and their sperm, yet we still come out as true-blue Deittoneans because the female injected whilst asleep is 80 percent genetically reared as Deittonean. The other percentage is them; they don't need much to make their mark and produce Deittonean-hybrid babies! It's all a subtle operation an' we get paid for our trouble!"

"So that's how it's done? How terrible! Does that mean your mother, and Estellene's mother were – you know!"

"Yup, that's so!"

"God, Rob! Are the other six the same?"

The 'other' six all shook their heads, as surprised as Janella was at Rob's revelation.

"Jesus, man," Tom looked disgustedly at Rob.

"Shit -don't glare at me like that! I can't help being a hybrid any mor'n that my wife can! These beings are not such demons as we make them out to be! They honestly want to help this world and create more hybrids to make our world a better place –"

"Only for themselves!" Janella cut in. "Rob, you've been fooled. These beings are cunning and love nothing more than mayhem and murder. They like to see misery. I sense it in their make-up. You were right to worry about your wife's supposed accident – I saw it happen in trance, although I didn't realize it at the time... The being materialized in the car beside her, startled her into driving off the road and crashing, breaking her pelvis! It was a warning for both of you not to get too entangled with your government job, or even me! They wanted to hurt your wife so you'd have to toe the line! They are evil! Please believe me! That casino bomb was planted by them, too, to maim you, and your wife's accident was instigated by them as some kind of warning I guess!"

"Mebbe so, but it won't wash, darling. We've been given so much – and looked after most of the time – why do you think I have so much tax money to spend? It all comes from them! It's all good shit!"

"It's blood money, man, dirty money!" Todd had now realized the truth. "They've paid you well for doing their terrible deeds!"

Ben and the others nodded their heads. "That's sounds about right!" Ben said. "We can't be matey with you any more, Rob; you've let us down!"

"Your all shits!" Rob found everyone was staring at him in disbelief. He straightened his shoulders and shrugged, saying laconically, as he walked away from them. "I like the money, okay? It was no big deal to use you Janella, you're a lovely lay! No hard feelings, huh?"

For an answer she strode up to him, and as he turned, she slapped his face once again. For rage-real this time! She was shaking with humiliation.

"How dare you and your capital leader use me like this! Its all been a bloody sham! I thought you loved me!"

"I do darling, but, as you've sussed, I love my wife equally too, and I'm still married to her, okay! Our marriage was a sham, darling!"

Her face was pinch-white, her teeth gummed together, her mouth in a grim straight line. In a smoldering rage she snarled bitingly: "So we were never married properly? You nasty, sneaky bastard! Just get out of my life now you son-of-a-bitch! I never want to see you again – here's your rings! It's over!"

She threw them fiercely far away. He didn't bother to pick them up.

He grinned lopsidedly. "Whatever happened to 'love'? I gave you a good time!"

Stung, a reply came, but only a bitter one. "I would dearly love to crack a gun over your head, but I don't do weapons!"

Tom came up, as Ben scathingly added: "We might be rug-rats chasing a skirt every night, but we're gentlemen compared with you! Leave her alone, McKen!"

Tom gently led her away, giving Rob a very black look. Tears were spilling down Janella's cheeks at her bust-up world.

Her guys gathered around her, trying to give her hurt pride some male comfort.

22

Hopgood-Royce sent out a large private hover-lear jet nicknamed 'Albatross' to pick them up. Also, extra ammunition was supplied to them. Janella found she'd been given a small silver pistol. To her instant surprise she seemed to know how to use it! It appeared her conscious realization of past demeanor was coming through to her psychic mind in the reality of now!

Rob McKen was given the cold shoulder by all his cronies, and on the journey back to the Capital, Janella sat rigidly apart from him, wondering where she could go to stay for the rest of night. She didn't want to go back to Pimlissa or Jaggard Mews.

Tom solved her problem. "We're all chipping in to place you in a good capital hotel for the next few nights. You don't want to go home to his house now, do you?"

"Definitely not."

"Okay, sweetheart, We'll be with you. You'll be safe. None of us had any idea Rob would turn traitor like this! I'm sorry for what he's put you through!"

"Oh, god, so am I!" She began to cry again.

Tom lifted her chin. "I'll see you okay now sweetheart!" He kissed her tear-y lips and hugged her tightly to him.

They went to Hotel Monglaizée in the French quarter of the capital, near to Hopgood-Royce's apartment – and Janella, heartbroken but head high, parted from Rob for good.

The one thing she did do, was to send her completed story to Hopgood-Royce's office so that he could get it out to the media, as had been planned. She knew the media would pass the news on instantly once it was eagerly received.

Janella's hero in the story, Jjoan Rivers, had shown a way of how to destroy the Lize-nard's presence. Janella hoped the one death of the 'colony king' as she called him, would help deplete and dispose the Lize-nard's power for good and give Deittoneans confidence in the future, as they continued to fight their foe with love and understanding, instead of with mass-produced weapons of war.

Brett had arranged with Rob to gather some of Janella's clothes from Jaggard Mews. Rob was going back to his Amisanean wife.

At the final parting, Rob spoke flatly to Janella's stiff back. "We had to get you in with us, as a hybrid mother. You're right; they would have killed my wife otherwise. Instead, they staged an accident for her. That's why I complied with Hopwood-Royce's plan to bring you in with me. It was lousy, but it worked. S'long Janella."

Stung again, she turned and faced him, eyes wide, making a flash guess. "I reckon Peter Hopgood-Royce is also one of you, a demoralized worker for the Lize-nards?"

"Nope. He was good; I was the bad guy through all the years our children were being brought up, because I knew what we were –an' I needed their tax chips to pay for our children's scholarships an' schooling. Hopgood-Royce sussed what I was, but thought I was helping him!"

"And you're wife let you do this? Knowing you let the Lize-nards kill people! You are a couple of money-grabbers aren't you! How dare you insult me by seeing me as a pawn in your plan, to use me as some kind of 'baby carrier' for the Lize-nard's! I'd rather die than do that, you're mad to even to think this of me!"

"It was worth a try!"

There was such a smirk on Rob's face that she nearly slapped him yet again. How could he have changed so much?

Tom led her away from the tense, bristling-with-rage confrontation, or she would have done so.

"C'mon baby, we have better things to do!"

They had all had luxurious showers in their own en-suite hotel rooms when they had a red alert from Hopgood-Royce. "I've passed your story onto our print office, Janella, but come here at once; our headquarters has been compromised by the Lize-nards. Where the hell's Rob – I can't contact him!"

"We've split – he's gone back to be with his darling wife in Amisana, and good riddance! I'm with the guys. We'll come at once!"

"Ah, I see, you've found out about Rob's er, complications shall we say? Ah, well, I'll speak to you later about that!"

"He didn't really love me! How can I create a story about loving the hybrid children if we get guys like Rob who think they have to toe the line and be in with the Lize-nards? I hate them for what they've done to our planet!"

"Janella, I know, but it's not so much the Lize-nards, but the hybrids that we must learn to love, and show them there is no shame in being one! Otherwise, there may be many suicides... Now, listen, tell your guys to bring their artillery. Quickly, we're all in mortal danger here! The Lize-nard's have broken in and taken some of my staff hostage – and I've got my back against the wall, bargaining with them. Your right, the bastards enjoy creating misery!" That was the last words he said. She heard a loud shot of some kind and, fearing the worst, ran out to tell the guys and galvanize them into action.

23

Fire and smoke were streaming from the lower doors and windows of the Capital building as Janella and her men reached the Capital where all-important decisions and conferences took place.

Peter Hopgood-Royce they found slumped against the wall of his oval office, bloody in the face and a hole in his heart. There were no security men or robots to be found anywhere!

"Oh no!" Janella cried for him. She'd liked the charismatic leader despite his dealing of her unusual occupation in her past. She happened to glance out of the shut oval window, biting her lip, and it seemed that even the trees outside seemed to bend their weather-singed tips in sympathy at the great leader's death.

Tom stayed with her whilst the others sussed out where the staff were. They were found in a back room, cringing with terror, when Todd opened their door, as they were expecting to see the Lize-nards.

The CL's personal secretary came forward nervously pushing his glasses back up his nose.

"Where's Peter Hopgood-Royce?"

"Dead, I'm afraid." Todd told him what had happened. He handed out guns to the secretary.

"Do you know how to handle these?"

"Not a clue how to use one! Peter's dead? They killed him? The ratty buggers!"

"Yeah. Let's get moving from here. Clay – can you take the women? We can't leave from the front, it's on fire, is there another way out?"

"Yes, I know of one!" The personal secretary brightened. "I can lead you. It's a secret room hidden below ground. I personally have the key to the door!"

Janella and tall Clay began to follow him out with the woman secretaries. Todd walked beside the man leading them, and Brett, Ben, Tom and Red brought up the rear carrying their firearms.

The personal secretary whose name was also Peter, led them all through a narrow tunnel which descended into stairs that went down and down. They all pattered down them holding onto the metal rail.

Janella, at the back, sensed something. "We're being followed, guys."

Tom stepped back and put a finger to his lips. Everyone – about ten in the crowd, stopped.

He listened, and spoke sot-to voice to Janella. "Carry on as quick as you can, me and Ben will stop these beings in their tracks!"

"Tom, be careful! Their dangerous!"

He crushed her too him and gave her a warm kiss and caressing smile. "We'll be careful! Okay Ben, ready?"

"Sure. We'll stop a few bastards!" Ben cocked his gun and stuck his chin out squarely and firmly. "They won't get past us! Carry on honey. See you on the other side!"

What he meant by that she wasn't sure, but smiled wanly and helped to move the others on again.

More stairs, then another narrow corridor and they came to a wide, strong, double-wielded iron door.

"Quick man," Todd urged, "get your key out!"

"It needs my eye and hand recognition as well. I'll have to take my glasses off."

Peter produced a large key from his left sock! He explained: "I grabbed it when they stormed Peter's oval room. I was next door and heard the shooting."

"Use it then!"

"Just a moment –" Peter placed his hand on the door, then eyed the lock. There was a whir and a red light gleamed through the hole of the lock. Satisfied, Peter then placed the key in the lock and it turned. The wielded door sprung open for them and they were in some kind of underground bunker complete with water, food and a second room that housed a toilet!

Suddenly, Janella whimpered, her hand to her mouth. She'd slipped into trance. Upstairs, she had seen Ben and Tom's bodies sprawled out on the staircase floor! She didn't know if they were dead or alive. She shuddered in horror.

Brett, Clay, Red and Todd surrounded her. "What's up?"

"Tom and Ben are down!"

Clay nodded sternly. "I'll go check it out. Get that door open again, Peter!"

"Er... I can't. It can only be opened from the other side – by me!"

Red glared at the personal secretary. "Are you telling us we're trapped down here!"

"Sorry – in the heat of the moment, I forgot that small matter!"

"SMALL!"

"I'm s-sorry – someone will come for us. Pat Brockly is the man who designed this get-up. I can call him on my hover-pad!"

"Do it, man, its essential we get outta here!" Red demanded.

"Oh, dear, his numbers flashing, but he's not answering... He must be away!"

"Oh god – how am I going to get to Tom!" Janella moaned.

"How are we gonna get out is more to the point!" Todd was trying to be practical.

There was a grating noise. Then a hammering on the closed door in front of them.

Then they heard the voice of a Lize-nard talking to them: "We know you are in there. This door may look strong, but we will soon break it down. Be prepared to die Deittoneans!"

The women secretaries all looked faintly at their rescuers, as scared as hell, and Janella's mind was in a turmoil wondering about Tom and Ben.

She went into a trance to try and locate them again, but instead, realised that once again, she was talking to Voldan who had visited her on board the Silver Star.

Voldan spoke to her mind. He was the only Lize-nard she knew who could do that, which, comfortingly, proved to her that he was not evil like the others were.

"My child, brain of my brain, I am with you and I will save you from my own kind. Listen to me now, do as I say quickly and calmly..."

She received his instructions and came out of trance, shouting urgently: "I know a way out; follow me!"

Before they could say anything, she'd opened the second door that housed the toilet. She pointed to the back of the cistern.

"There is an escape chute behind here. We file out quickly, one-by-one."

The personal secretary gaped at her in amazement. "How do you know this? Have you been here before?"

"I can't explain now," she was tugging at the back of the cistern and had found some kind of spring-lock. She clicked it and an aperture opened to reveal lights coming on in an underground facility.

"Follow me!" She dived through it. Without hesitation, everyone followed.

Behind them, the big door to their new-found sanctuary was buckling inwards and the Lize-nards were coming through...

24

The underground facility had many passageways opening up to them. No one except Janella knew which way to go, thanks to Voldan's minute instructions.

"Bear left," she said, and left they went.

"How do you know the way Miss?" A perplexed personal secretary Peter asked her.

"I'm a trance psychic; my mentor is showing me the way out!"

"But, who is your mentor?"

"Voldan. He is leading me by my mind!"

Peter shrugged, at a loss to ask this strange woman who 'Voldan' was!

The boys knew and they hurried up the rest of the group, for they could hear worrying echoes and sounds behind them, quite close...

"Right, now..." Janella stood still. "You all go through this passageway, then out into the road that's opposite the Capital building. By now the fire people should be there. You can stay safe with them. I'm going back for Tom and Ben!"

"Janella, you can't!" Brett was instantly beside her trying to hold her back. He saw her baby silver pistol was now held in her hand.

She shook her head stubbornly. "I love Tom, and I owe him for saving me from Rob's grandiose plans."

He could see she meant it. "I'll come with you!"

Tall Clay turned to the people they'd escorted through the labyrinth of tunnels. "The way is clear for you to escape. Go now and bring back help; we're all going back with Janella."

There were cries of dissent, but he shooed the people on, then turned to Janella. "Like it or not, we're coming with you honey."

She grinned wanly. "I'm happy to have your fire-power. We'll thrash 'em on the way!"

But it was too late. Three Lize-ards had traversed the last of the tunnel and were entering the bay where the four of them stood. They had woody club-like weapons that were being charged up in scaly hands.

"Stand your ground Deittoneans. Throw down your arms!"

The group had no choice but to do so.

In her mind, Janella called out to Voldan. "Help us Voldan!"

She didn't even have to invoke a trance, suddenly he was there, right beside her, in being, in the physical sense, as it were. There was some kind of vest strapped onto his chest, but he seemed to carry no weapons.

She had spoken of Voldan to all her men, but Clay and Brett looked astonished at seeing him in real time. Both of them showed their alarm by grouping themselves around Janella.

Voldan looked into her eyes reassuringly. He spoke forcefully and urgently. "Leave me now, Janella, but draw on who you were. I will give you a memory to show what you were to me, and to yourself – remember it!" She saw a picture form in his palm, and she gasped.

"I – I'm not – oh, please – dear god, no!"

It was the machine picture he hadn't allowed her to see. This time, she understood.

Her boys were gaping at her quizzically. She motioned them to move as quickly as she herself was now doing. They left Voldan facing his own people as they hurried away, following a shocked Janella out into the street that was opposite the fired capital building.

Left alone, tall and menacing, his red eyes flashing, Voldan looked his kinsmen in the eye. He growled, "Remember me, Asdon?"

He appealed to the group leader, the being who stood in the middle of the three Lize-nards. "You created me Asdon – only you know what I am! What are you going to do about it?"

The Lize-nard being in front of Voldan scowled. "Then I will have to un-create you! Sleep forever Voldan – you traitorous robot! You have ruined us!" He pointed his weapon at Voldan just as Voldan slapped a button on his vest.

As Janella and her male friends emerged into the street, there followed a terrific explosion from the escape hatch and smoke billowed out. In another trance she realized Voldan had blown himself up, killing the others of his kind with him.

She was instantly sad about that, yet her thoughts were already jumping elsewhere.

"TOM!" In her agonized mind she supposed Tom and Ben had been blown up as well.

She started to move back into the smoky wreckage of their passageway.

Brett quickly stopped her from running back with a reassuring grin. "It's okay Janella. Don't go there! You don't have to! Look who's coming round the corner in one piece!"

And there he was, with Ben limping beside him: "TOM! TOM! Ben! - OH!" Janella ran towards them both. She rushed straight into Tom's arms, trying to hug Ben at the same time!

"How the hell did you survive that, Tom?"

Tom gave a laconic answer from a smudged, dust-smeared face and hair. "We were knocked down, but we got up again! Don't worry – we're fine! Your friend Voldan, he's been blown to smithereens."

"Yeah, I know, along with those wicked Lize-nards who were following us. I think their leader's dead! I don't think the other Lize-nards will stay now its all out in the open, and they know we'll be helping the lize-nard offspring to adjust to any shame they may feel being hybrids!"

Everyone in her group nodded.

Yet, even as she hugged Tom, she remembered Voldan's picture framed on his hand for the last time, showing her who she was...

The screen image had depicted him being designed as a robot by the Lize-nards scientists and engineers, and in turn she realized, that he had shown her that she was a robot too! There she was, all down through the centuries as flesh and blood! But Voldan had recreated her for the 22nd Century in a different way, just like he'd tried to explain to her, and she hadn't understood it all then.

In a sense her 'Beastkiller' story had come true. Hadn't Stacey been a robot too? Deep down in her consciousness she must have known this about herself – how strange! Voldan had left her with the memory of how she had been made for this century only.

Finally, the truth was out. She had found herself, and because of this she was feeling paradoxically happy and free! Such knowledge had released her inner self. She knew she had consciousness and a soul, and that that had never been lost to her, but had stayed with her down through all the centuries.

In a flash of understanding she realized all her life-long training for this moment in time. Even the fact that in this century she had been a man's women to several men, without suspecting it!

As intimate as she'd been with Rob and the boys, they hadn't sussed out a thing!

That she was really a robot!

It was still too much to take in yet, and she thought: "I'll never tell anyone, except maybe Tom." But would he accept and understand this? She hoped so, but wasn't too sure.

Voldan may have created her in his robotic likeness, but his knowledge of how he'd done it to her had died with him, and she realized, as a robot, she could never have children.

As she hugged Tom to her, delighted beyond delight that he was alive she resolved she wouldn't tell a soul! Not even Tom.

And Tom's first words to her were: "Phew, Janella, let's get outta this heat-stricken Capital City. I fancy living with you somewhere underwater, where it's cooler!"

Janella beamed at him. "I know just the place!" She said. "Come with me, Tom! We'll start a new life together, in a private dwelling in Farseisia – all of you guys will be welcome to come and visit us! Is that all right, Tom?"

"Yeah – but no sharing this time round! You guys go and find your own dames! I'm going t'stay 'visible' for Janella's sake now!"

"Wow, Tom, I second that!" and Janella squeezed his dust-covered hand, radiantly happy. She vaguely heard someone in her group say: "Lucky Tom!" But that was all.

THE END